4. 6 AR/
7.0 pts.

VOYAGE OF ICE

MICHELE  TORREY

VOYAGE OF ICE

CHRONICLES OF COURAGE

Alfred A. Knopf
New York

$\mathcal{V}$OYAGE OF $\mathcal{I}$CE

Being the true story of my, Nicholas Robbins',

experience aboard the whaleship SEA HAWK,

and of my captain's cruelty,

our shipwreck in the Arctic,

and of the hardships suffered thereby.

As told to
MICHELE TORREY

THE WHALE is a beautiful creature, with the heart and spirit of a true giant. It is this author's dream that the commercial whale fishery become a relic of a bygone era, used only as a tool of enlightenment, so that the oceans will again be filled with the varied species of this magnificent beast for generations to come.

THIS IS A BORZOI BOOK PUBLISHED BY ALFRED A. KNOPF

www.randomhouse.com/kids

Library of Congress Cataloging-in-Publication Data
Torrey, Michele.
Voyage of ice / by Michele Torrey. — 1st ed.
    p.   cm.
SUMMARY: In 1851, fifteen-year-old Nick and his older brother, longing to be whalers, sign on as hands on the whaling ship Sea Hawk, and find that the journey is full of hardship and unexpected dangers.
ISBN 0-375-82381-6 (trade) — ISBN 0-375-92381-0 (lib. bdg.)
[1. Whaling—Fiction. 2. Brothers—Fiction. 3. Seafaring life—Fiction. 4. Survival—Fiction. 5. Arctic regions—Fiction. 6. Adventure and adventurers—Fiction.] I. Title.
PZ7.T645725Vo 2004
[Fic]—dc22
2003060407

Printed in the United States of America

May 2004

10 9 8 7 6 5 4 3 2 1

First Edition

To Elizabeth,
a true lady

⧖

Out of whose womb came the ice?
And the hoary frost of Heaven, who hath gendered it?
The waters become hard like stone,
And the face of the deep is frozen.

—Job 38:29-30

The day my father returned from the sea, I was five years old. It was a day like any other. Blue skies dotted with clouds, sea-gulls floating on the breeze, me peering through my spyglass.

The year was 1842, and my older brother, Dexter, and I lived with our aunt Agatha in a considerable grand mansion on County Street. From the glass-enclosed cupola atop our home, I could see down the hill, past our town of New Bedford, Massachusetts, and to the river. Dozens of ships lay alongside the wharves, their masts and yards like a jumble of spilled toothpicks.

There were always ships a-coming and a-going. I didn't know which was my father's; after all, he'd been gone since before I could remember. But every day I watched anyways, sometimes running down the steps to fetch my aunt, pulling her by the sleeve, asking her to come look through my spyglass and tell me whether this ship was *the one*. Aunt Agatha would look, sigh, say no, hand back my spyglass, and tell me not to bother her again, for she had a garden to tend and raspberry jam to put by.

On this day, though, my aunt fetched me. I turned, and there she stood, wiping her floury hands on her apron, with Dexter beside her. She brushed a wisp of salt-and-pepper hair out of her eyes, leaving a white smudge on her temple. "Your father's ship is here."

I wanted to dash to the waterfront, not even stopping to put on my shoes. Aunt Agatha not only made me put on my shoes, but made me wash my face, scrub behind my ears, and then walk beside Dexter and behave proper. Dexter's whisper tickled my ear. "Do you think Father will like us?" Dexter was seven years old, and I couldn't imagine anyone not liking him. Everyone liked Dexter. As for me, I liked Dexter as well as I liked custard pudding. Maybe better.

I started to answer, to tell Dexter I liked him better than pudding, but Aunt Agatha yanked his arm, then rapped the back of my head. "Hush now."

Long before we arrived at the wharf, a warm breeze wafted from the waterfront, thick with whale oil, fresh-cut oak, and pitch. Then, finally, we were there, standing beside my father's ship. My heart beat wild. He was here! Finally here! I kept pointing to the different men who disembarked, tugging on my aunt's skirt. "Is that him? Is he my father?"

"Hush. You'll know soon enough, I expect. And stop that jumping. Ye make my teeth rattle."

And then there he was. I near burst with joy. "Dexter! Nicholas! Right smart, lively children you be!" He laughed and swung us both onto his shoulders. He was thin and tall as a ship's mast, or very nearly, anyways, and so it was a great thing to be atop his shoulder. He smelled of the sea, of salt, and of the wind.

That night, when he tucked me into bed, he handed me a gift. "This is for you. Carved it myself, I did."

It looked like a horn, curved and whitish yellow. On it was carved a picture of Father's ship. I looked at him, wondering. "'Tis a tooth from the mighty sperm whale," he explained, "a monster fish so ferocious it can swallow a soul in a single gulp; it can crush a ship and eat all her sailors and still be hungry."

"Have you killed a sperm whale?"

"Aye. Many. 'Tis what lights our lamps and makes our candles. Nothing burns so bright and white as sperm oil."

I hugged the tooth, vowing to keep it forever. "It's grand," I said, "and you are very brave." That night I dreamed I battled a whale. He thrashed his mighty tail and smashed my boat to splinters, but not before my lance pierced his vitals.

Day after day we strolled through the city streets, my father, Dexter, and I, over the cobblestones and under the elms, past other stately mansions and into the city center. Past the apothecary, the livery stable, the blacksmith's shop. Father tipped his hat to folks, saying, "How be you, Widow Taber?" or "How be you today, Reverend Wood?"

Always they replied, "'Twas a fine, greasy voyage ye made, Cap'n Robbins. All the folks be talking 'bout it." Then they pinched my cheeks, shook Dexter's hand, and looked fair pleased to see us.

"Why," said one woman, "but don't Dexter look like his mother used to, God rest her soul, what with his sandy hair, eyes the color of molasses, and a smile that takes my breath away. Handsome as a hackman's hat, he is."

"The girls will be pining after him before too many years," said another.

"And my stars and body, don't your other boy look just like you, Cap'n Robbins! Eyes like shamrocks, and thin as a splinter, he is! Tall as a steeple too."

"Why, how proud ye must be, Cap'n Robbins."

Three months later, my father left to hunt whales again, aboard the *Africa*. I waved good-bye, sobbing, thinking I would be eight or maybe even nine years old before I saw him next. Each morning after, no sooner did my eyes pop open than I raced to the cupola and peered through the spyglass, the carved tooth beside me on the windowsill, vowing to watch every day until he returned. Every day I imagined him poised in the bow of his whaleboat, battling the sperm whale, thrusting his lance until the great beast lay still. A mighty hunter. My father.

But not all my life was spent in the cupola. No indeed. Aunt Agatha wouldn't stand for it any more than she'd stand for dirty ears or picking your nose at the table. "You'll turn pale as a worm," she said. "Boys are meant to be boys. Run along now. Scat."

So, month after month, come afternoon, Dexter and I would meander to the waterfront and sneak aboard the ships with our school friends. Aloft in the ratlines we scrambled, out on the yards, lazy as you please. Or we'd climb way, way up to the masthead lookout station. Whenever we spied the telltale spout, we'd holler, *"There she blo-o-o-ows!"* The sailors gave us treats. The mates told us to get down. The captains said, "Come back in a few years, boys. I'll make ye rich as Midas and greasy as a hog." And they clapped us on our backs and sent us on our way.

Dexter could climb higher than anyone, knew his knots and all the right cuss words. I was real proud of him. "That's my brother," I said to the sailors one day. "He knows all the right cuss words." The sailors winked at each other and nodded serious-like. Then they taught me a few cuss words Dexter didn't know yet.

That evening when Aunt Agatha told me to set the table for supper, I tried out one of my new cuss words on her. Judging by the soapsuds foaming out of my mouth for the next day or so, it was a right nasty word. Certain, I'd make a fine sailor someday. Then, after I was a sailor, a whaling captain.

Tall, smiling, and smelling of the wind.

The summer day stretched before us like freedom. We lay atop a rock, Dexter and I, sunning ourselves. We'd spent the afternoon here on Palmer's Island, running and hiding among the old cedars and craggy rocks. First we'd played Indians, then pirates. Now we played lizards.

A fly buzzed round my face and I blinked slow-like. I chewed on a stalk of grass. "Where do you suppose he is now?"

"Who?"

"Father." I glanced at Dexter. A stalk of grass poked out of the side of his mouth. Summer streaked his sandy hair. A few freckles were sprinkled across his nose like cinnamon.

He shrugged. "I dunno. Somewheres."

"When do you suppose he's coming home?"

"I dunno."

"Do you miss him?"

He shrugged again. "I expect."

I propped myself up on one elbow, wondering if lizards did the same. "I'm going to be a whaling captain when I grow up, just like Father."

"Me too."

A warm breeze wafted over me and I lay back down. The sky stretched blue from one end of the horizon to the other. I imagined being aboard a ship, lying on the deck and staring at the sky. And after I finished staring at the sky, I'd stare at the sea. No matter where I stared, there'd be nothing but blue. "We'll be on the same ship."

"There's only one captain allowed on a ship."

I frowned. There must be a way we could be on the ship at the same time. "Then we'll take turns being captain."

An easy smile played across Dexter's face. "Aye. But I'll be first." He sat up suddenly. "C'mon. This is boring. Let's play captains."

First Dexter played Captain Nye, who got his leg chewed off by a sperm whale but killed the whale anyways. Then I played Captain Coffin, who gave all the sailors a raise and a treat because they caught a whale, but who afterward bravely went down with his ship.

The sun was sinking. The sky burned orange. I was in the middle of drowning when I saw something lying under a tree. Something alive. I hurried over and gathered it up. "What did you find?" Dexter asked from behind me, panting because he'd been drowning too.

"A baby bird." It was pink and featherless, and its purplish eyes were still closed. I saw its heart beating beneath the skin.

"Put it down. It's hopeless."

I stroked it with my little finger. "But it hasn't even lived its life yet."

Dexter peered into the tree overhead. "Must've fallen from

its nest. C'mon, Nick, put it down. It'll make a fine meal for something."

A lump like cold, day-old porridge formed in my throat. Dexter was always bossing me around. I tried to keep my chin from quivering. "But we can't let it die."

"All things die, Nick."

"I can feed it milk. And a worm, maybe."

He sighed, shrugged. "Fine. Suit yourself. But don't come crying to me when Aunt Agatha busts your hide for bringing it in the house."

I rushed to the rowboat. The hatchling was warm in my hands, and all the way back I whispered to it while Dexter rowed the boat and rolled his eyes.

At home, I didn't tell Aunt Agatha but hurried to the cupola. For two days I kept the bird alive, but it finally died as Dexter said it would. I held the cold, stiff body, thinking maybe it wasn't really dead yet, but Dexter snatched it from me and buried it in a hole in the yard. "It's over," he said, dry-eyed and looking disgusted.

I bawled my eyes out. Couldn't help it. I visited the little grave for weeks, until it was overgrown and I could no longer see where it used to be.

Two years, four months, and twenty-six days after our father left, a man came to our house. Tall and unsmiling he was, and dressed in black. He stood on the doorstep crushing his wide-brimmed hat in his hands until Aunt Agatha invited him in for a cup of tea and a biscuit or two. He sat in the parlor and put his hat on his knee. The clock ticked on the mantel. In the distance, I heard the clop-clop of horses' hooves and the crunch of wheels.

While Aunt Agatha went to fetch tea and biscuits, Dexter sat beside me on the piano bench. Together we studied the man. "Maybe he's from school," Dexter whispered, accidentally plunking the piano with his elbow. "Maybe they're holding you back a year because you're stupid and still can't read."

"Maybe he has news of Father. Maybe he knows when Father will be home and how many barrels of oil the *Africa* has taken. Thousands, maybe."

"Or maybe he's here to ask for Aunt Agatha's hand in marriage. Maybe they're . . . *lovers.*"

Aunt Agatha? Married? What a ridiculous thought! As ridiculous as kissing a girl and pretending you liked it. We stifled our smiles and sat up straight when Aunt Agatha entered the room carrying a tray.

Just then, the stranger spoke. His voice fell into the silence like a rock dropped into a still pond. It about stopped my heart. "Perhaps 'twould be better if the boys left the room."

Aunt Agatha blinked, and I could have sworn she paled. Then the lines on her face turned hard. She set the tray on a table. "Dexter, Nicholas, go to the cupola. I'll fetch ye when 'tis time."

At first we didn't budge, but when she said, "Go now," in her special voice that meant *You'd better behave or I'll give ye a taste of switch pie,* we both hurried out of the room, closing the door behind us. Halfway up the stairs, Dexter stopped. "Let's listen anyways."

We pressed our ears to the door. I could hear the thump of my heart, Dexter breathing beside me, his eyes wide.

The man was speaking. I caught snatches of his conversation. ". . . the *Africa* . . . Captain Robbins . . . God rest his soul . . . lost at sea . . . a bull whale gone mad . . . dashed to pieces . . ."

I didn't wait to hear more. Without a word, I fled. Out the door, down the hill, my lungs bursting, past the wharves to the shore. I collapsed on the riverbank. Then the tears came. Flowing into the grass, into the soil.

After a while, I rolled over, my face to the sky. Dexter was beside me. I didn't know how long he'd been there. "Don't cry, Nick," he said, his voice breaking. "Don't cry." But he lay down too and we stared at the sky for a long, long time.

CHAPTER
2

*S*ix and a half years later, on a brisk October morning in 1851 when the wind gusted through the trees and the leaves swirled to the ground, Dexter and I became whalemen.

I buttoned my pea jacket tight, snugged my cap down, shoved my hands in my pockets, and walked the sailor walk, jaunty and swaggering. I strolled along next to Dexter, taller than him by half a head. Ship after ship, wharf after wharf, seeming miles, reeking of oil and the sea. The air resounded with the bang of hammers, the boom of coopers' mallets, and the rasp of grindstones. Oxcarts rumbled over the wharves. Mountains of casks covered the docks.

"Looking to be whalemen?" A recruiter sat behind a table, pen in hand, smiling. Gold teeth glinted.

I glanced at the ship behind him. She looked right shabby, her timbers worn. She needed new paint and fresh canvas. "Thanks, but no," said Dexter. We turned away.

"Young men like you ought to make fine harponeers. 'Tis an easy life. 'Twill make ye a fortune."

"No, thank you," we said together, walking on.

"She may look shabby, but she's seaworthy," the man hollered after us. "Been afloat for eighty year now. Couldn't sink her with a hundred cannon. And the captain's a generous, kindly man. Ask anybody. Pays top dollar for men like you. 'Tis the opportunity of a lifetime."

"Probably crawling with bugs," I said as we kept walking. Rotch's Wharf, Central Wharf, Taber's Wharf. All the recruiters calling at us to join them. It was fun, and I swelled with importance.

Suddenly, Dexter stopped as if he'd hit a wall. He stared goggle-eyed at a ship, and I swear I saw drool drip from his lip. "She's the one I've been dreaming about all these years, Nick. She's a beauty."

Aye, she was a beauty, all right. Three-masted, bark-rigged, with fresh black paint and shiny new copper sheathing, the *Sea Hawk* of New Bedford looked right sharp and ready to sail.

"Sign here, young fellows, don't just stand a-gawking," said the *Sea Hawk*'s recruiter, holding out his pen for us. The recruiter was large, blubbery, as if he'd had a few too many roly-poly puddings. "Sign here for the time of your lives. Whaling will make ye rich. You'll never have to work again."

"Does it have bugs?" I asked.

"Not a one. Clean as an angel's sheets. Cap'n Thorndike wouldn't have it any other way."

"Good. I hate bugs."

With a swagger Dexter grabbed the pen and signed his name.

"My brother Nick here's fifteen today." He straightened and patted his coat pocket. "Our aunt signed a letter of permission. Said we both had to wait until Nick turned fifteen, and today's the day. Said we had to go together or not at all. Says I've got to take care of him, me being the older brother and all."

"Ah!" The recruiter turned his gaze to me. "'Tis your good fortune to meet with the *Sea Hawk* on your birthday, lad. 'Twill bring ye good greasy luck." He held out the pen. "Go ahead, then. Sign on the line there.

"Well, then, ah—Nicholas and Dexter Robbins," said the recruiter, peering at the contract we'd just signed, "let's have your letter of permission. Makes things easier all round."

"Our father was a whaling captain," I said as Dexter handed him the letter. "He started whaling when he was sixteen. He was killed by a whale, though. Dashed his boat to pieces. We're going to be whaling captains just like him."

"That so? That so? Ain't that interesting now." Scarcely glancing at the letter, he set it aside, heaved himself to his feet, and held out his hand. "Looks like everything's in fine order. Welcome aboard the *Sea Hawk,* lads. She sails in the morning."

We shook his hand, neither of us able to stop grinning. By fire, we were going a-whaling!

The *Sea Hawk* was away, courses and headsails filled with the stiff autumn breeze. Down the Acushnet River, past Palmer's Island, and through Buzzards Bay we sailed.

The mates barked orders. Men sprang to obey. Someone cursed at me and told me to steer clear. Another laughed, saying, "Green as seaweed, he is." I felt myself blush, wishing that I was already an old salt, but knowing I was just like the other greenies—easy to spot in stiff new dungarees. All day the mates kept us greenies hopping, ordering us high atop the yards to reef the

sails, hollering whenever they needed someone to yank a rope. I
was good at yanking ropes. Dexer too. We grinned at each other
across many a rope.

"Here we are," he'd say, breathing hard.

"Just like we always dreamed."

Only a few of the men did I recognize—a couple of the
mates, men who'd hollered at me many times in years past to get
down from the yards, afterward patting my head. Good men, I
knew, who had families and went to church Sundays, who tipped
their hats to Aunt Agatha as we passed in the streets. Everyone
else, some thirty men or so, was a stranger.

Come dusk, as the last of the land fell astern, the first mate
called us amidships. The other three mates stood at the rail,
watching us foremast hands in the waning light, saying nothing
as we gathered round the main hatch. A goat bleated. The air
stank of tobacco and cabbages. A side of beef hung from the
amidship shelter and moved like a pendulum as the ship rose and
fell on the ocean swells. My body ached; my hands were raw and
red. I'd left my dinner behind in Buzzards Bay. I hoped they
would let us go rest now that we were at sea. Now that the hard
work was over.

A cockroach scurried by and I jumped. *By fire, I hate bugs! I
thought the* Sea Hawk *didn't have bugs!* Dexter saw me jumping
and calmly ground it beneath his brogan.

Still we stood round, no one saying anything. Where was the
captain? I'd yet to see him, and wondered what kind of man he
was. Was he kindly, like the other captains I'd met? Was he like
my father? I thought to tell him that the *Sea Hawk* had a bug
problem.

Off to the side, the four harponeers lounged lazy. One
sprawled atop a crate of potatoes, picking his teeth. Smug, they
were. A breed apart. I knew that not only did the harponeers

bunk in steerage rather than the fo'c'sle, but they earned more money and were tough fellows.

Then the captain appeared. He was a big bully of a man, strong-jawed and barrel-chested. A deep, jagged scar stretched from his neck over his left cheek and disappeared into a depression in his scalp. His eyes were gray, like the sky. Hard, like rocks.

Jerusalem crickets, I thought, *he could snap me in two with his bare hands!* Dexter and I glanced at one another. He looked a little unsure, as if maybe we'd been a mite hasty signing aboard the *Sea Hawk*.

The captain paced in front of us, his hands clasped behind his back. His voice booming like thunder. "I am Captain Ebenezer Thorndike of the *Sea Hawk*. Men, we be here for one reason only: to fetch a cargo of oil. You greenies have one week to learn the ropes. As for all of ye, there'll be no sleeping on your watches, no fighting, no grumbling, no wasting grub, no drinking, and no shirking of your duties. You'll respect the officers and give no back talk."

Suddenly, he stopped pacing and looked at each of us in turn. I tried not to look scared out of my wits when he stared hard at me. "Now, I'm an easygoing man. Easy so long as ye follow my orders and look lively. But cross me, men, and you'll find me made of sterner stuff altogether. I'll not hesitate to use the lash, lock ye in irons, or hang ye up by your thumbs. I've done it before, and 'tis my right to do so again." His eyes narrowed and his voice turned leaden. "Cross me, men, and this will become a hell ship. That's all I've got to say."

Having said his piece, the captain walked aft and disappeared down the companionway.

Then, before I could shut my flapping mouth, or whisper to Dexter that we were goners for certain and it had been nice knowing him, the four mates strolled down the line of foremast hands, sixteen of us in all.

"Take off your coat and let me see your muscles."

"Ever pull in a boat? No? Worthless, good-for-nothing trash! What did you come for, then? Hoping to travel the world?"

"What? I can't understand a word you're saying. On this ship we speak English. *Comprenez-vous?* We speak English!"

"Flex your arm. Show me your hands. Why, ye ain't never done a lick of work in your miserable life! What did ye think—ye were a-going on holiday?"

"How old be ye? Seventeen! Why, if I didn't know better, I'd say ye be a liar. Ye still talk like a girl."

The fourth mate prodded a boy next to me. The boy looked round eighteen years old. Orange-haired, freckled, green-eyed, teeth white as milk. "Ever look an angry whale in the eye, farm boy? Eh? Speak up!"

"Yes, sir!"

"What ship and for how long?"

"The *Alabaster,* sir, and for two years, sir!"

"What position?"

"Tub oarsman, sir!"

"Ever darted an iron at a whale?"

"Once, sir!"

"And?"

"I—I missed, sir!"

Suddenly, the first mate barked in my face. "How old be ye?"

I blinked and my stomach shriveled into a knot. *Why, I know him—he's Alexander Cole, one of the mates who acted friendly-like when Dexter and I were children.* Only he didn't seem so friendly all of a sudden. He was short and squat, his brown hair sticking straight up like a brush. "Fifteen, sir!"

"Green as the hills, ain't ye?"

"Yes, sir!"

"Never done a lick of work in your life, have ye?"

"Yes, sir—I mean—no, sir!"

"Take off your coat, greenie."

I whipped off my pea jacket. Cole grabbed my arm and yanked it toward him. "By thunder," he snarled. "If this ain't the most pathetic arm I've seen in all me whaling days. Ain't an ounce of muscle." He dropped my arm. Then, with his face just two inches from my own, veins bulging, he roared, "How do ye expect to pull an oar with just your bones, eh, Bones?"

"I'll do my best, sir!"

He grunted and moved on, screaming at Dexter an inch from Dexter's face as saliva flew from his mouth. "What are ye standing there looking like an idiot for? Take off your blasted coat so I can have a look at your muscles!"

"Yes, sir!" Dexter quickly shrugged off his coat.

"Ever pull in a boat, greenie?"

"No, sir! I mean, yes, sir! To—uh—Palmer's Island, sir!"

"Palmer's Island? Why, even babies do that! What good are ye to us, then? Whale bait, maybe? At least you'd come in handy!"

"Yes, sir! I'll do everything I can to catch a whale, sir!"

The mate's eyes narrowed. "Why, if I didn't know better, I'd say you've never seen a whale before, have ye?"

Dexter licked his lips. "Uh—no, sir. I hear they're very big, though."

Cole reeled backward and punched his own forehead. "Blast me eyes, if we come home with more than a barrel of oil in less than ten years, it'll be a miracle."

Finally, the mates finished looking us over. One by one, beginning with First Mate Cole, they began calling names. The red-haired fellow was chosen by the fourth mate. Dexter was also chosen by the fourth mate; he said he liked Dexter's hustle. I was the last left leaning against the rail. None of the mates looked as if they wanted to choose me. Me, a greenie, not very quick on his feet, only fifteen, with no muscles to speak of. *Bones.* I stared straight ahead, my face hot as a blister.

The fourth mate sighed. "Blast it, greenie, I always get the leftovers. You're with me."

I never worked so hard in my life.

There were scores of tasks to do. Spurred on by the mates, we worked like madmen getting ready for whaling. "For what if a huge sperm whale passes in front of our bow, and us not ready?" said the second mate. "Captain Thorndike will nail your hides to the masts."

There was cutting tackle to rig, a cutting stage to construct. Four whaleboats to prepare with oars, rigging, and sails. We stretched out whaleline, removed the kinks, and coiled it in tubs. The harponeers sharpened their lances and harpoons from dawn till dusk. I heard the stony rasp of whetting metal even in my sleep. Strangely, sometimes after nightfall I thought I heard piano music. Bach or Mozart or some such.

All that first week we greenies were drilled on the ropes and boxing the compass. My head swam and I broke into a sweat whenever someone asked me a question or gave me an order. Dexter hopped to every task with a mind to outwork us all. When orders were given to trim sail, he was the first up the rat-lines. Already he was a better sailor than I was, remembering everything as if it were easy, as if he'd done this all his life. *Why is everything so hard for me?* I thought. *Why can't I be like Dexter— handsome, smart, living life like it was made just for me?*

One day I headed aft, past the tryworks, past the duck and chicken coops, to fetch our dinner from the galley. Cook put the food in a tub or two, and today it was my turn to bring my shipmates their grub. I was just past the steerage companionway when I saw a girl. *What in tunket?* I craned my neck as I walked. With a cat cradled in her arms, she leaned against the rail, her corn-silk blond hair blowing round as she gazed out to sea.

By fire. There's a girl aboard the Sea Hawk.

*S*he must have felt my gaze, because she turned and looked at me with eyes blue as Aunt Agatha's cornflowers. My heart flip-flopped. *She's my age. And pretty as a posy.*

A smile played at the corners of her lips. Our gazes locked for the briefest moment before I crashed headlong into the galley door. *Dad blamedest!* I heard her laugh. Cook opened the door. "What the—"

"Sorry, Cook."

"Stupid greenie. Watch where you're a-going."

I looked back to where the girl had been, but she was gone, cat and all.

"Ah, ye ain't the first one who's gone goggle-eyed over her." Cook wiped his hands on his apron. "The captain catches you staring, though, he'll rip out your eyes and fry 'em for supper."

"Who—who is she?"

"Why, she's Elizabeth, the captain's daughter, who else?" he answered, loading my arms with the tub.

Thorndike's daughter!

"Lived her whole life at sea. Fifteen years, or thereabouts. Born aboard ship, she was. Takes her school lessons from her mother most days. Now, Mrs. Thorndike's some picky, doesn't like cabbage or pickled meat, likes tea 'stead of coffee, and that stuff's expensive, mind! She's a regular genteel lady. They both are. Go on now. The fellows be waiting."

"She's a looker," whispered Dexter one day. "All the guys are talking about her."

The two of us stood at the lookout station, one on each side of the mast. A single iron hoop circled each of us, chest high. Dexter leaned against his hoop and gazed aft to where Elizabeth sat sipping tea with her mother, a tall, spare woman who dressed in black.

Mostly, Elizabeth and Mrs. Thorndike stayed aft, near the captain's quarters, seldom venturing even as far as the mainmast. And except to fetch grub from the galley or to take a trick at the helm, we sailors rarely went abaft, as that was "officers' country." But looking aft was free.

"Who, Mrs. Thorndike?" Like Dexter, I whispered soft as no talking was allowed on lookout.

Dexter glanced at me as if I were nuts.

I looked away, out over the ocean, the breeze catching my hair, a tight feeling in my chest.

"By fire, little brother, if I didn't know better, I'd say you have a crush on Miss Elizabeth. Well, you'd better not do anything about it. I mean, blood and thunder, she's the captain's daughter! That's like being the daughter of Ivan the Terrible or something. We touch, we die."

It doesn't matter, I thought, irritated that Dexter always seemed to know what I was thinking and always told me what to do. *All I'm doing is looking anyways.*

Day after day, the seas remained empty.

Some days we backed the sails and went a-whaling—or at least pretended to. Each of the four whaleboats was thirty feet long, pointed at both ends so it could sail in either direction. If in close quarters with a whale, the rudder was drawn up and a steering oar was used, making it possible for the boat to turn quickly on its own length. Our boat, the starboard quarter boat, was crammed with six of us and half a ton of equipment. After rowing hard that first day, I had blisters the size of pancakes.

Occasionally a log was thrown into the water and we took turns tossing the harpoon. Of course, during a real chase, only the harponeer would dart the harpoon, but it was good training. I struck several times, and was glad when the fourth mate, Henry Sweet, clapped me on the back and said, "Well done. I guess them bones of yours be good for more than just clacking together."

After one month at sea, we were nearing the equator, and the weather had turned considerable warm even though it was late November. One day during the second dogwatch, from six to eight in the evening, all hands except the helmsman lounged round the windlass in clusters, smoking and yarning. I played backgammon with Dexter.

"You see, Bones, they been fished out," said Garret Hix, the red-haired farm boy from Illinois. We called him Carrot Sticks. He was a fine fellow.

I moved a piece. "Fished out?"

"Aye," said an older sailor, tattooed and sun-hardened. He carved off a wedge from a slab of tobacco and pressed it inside his cheek. "Days were when ye couldn't sail a ship without bumping into a sperm whale. Practically begged ye to take them. Now 'tis like finding a fart in a hurricane. Friend of mine went a year without seeing one. Eyes dried to raisins from a-staring so hard."

"A year," I breathed. I knew the *Sea Hawk*'s voyage would not end until her hold burst with whale oil. To go a whole year without one barrel . . .

"That's why we're headed to the Arctic." Garret lay on his back, picking his teeth with a toothpick.

Dexter looked at me, his expression confused.

"The Arctic?" I asked. "Where's that?"

"Och!" exclaimed an Irishman we called Irish. "Even for a greenie, he's daft as a brush. One brick short of a load, so he is."

I blushed, though it wasn't the first time I'd been teased about not knowing something. It was the fate of every greenie, I expect.

Garret propped himself up on his elbow, the toothpick dangling from his mouth. He looked at me blank, as if he hadn't realized before how daft I was. "Well, it's up north about as far as you can get without heading south again. It's frozen cold and full of ice."

"And we're going there?" *Frozen cold? Ice?*

Dexter said nothing, bending his head over the game board.

"I thought you knowed," said Garret.

"But then why are we headed south?" I asked, feeling ignorant but wanting answers.

"Well, you see, Bones, we've got to sail round Cape Horn before we can head north to the Arctic. There's a continent in our way, you know."

More grins.

"But I don't understand. Why would we even want to go there? To the Arctic, I mean?"

"What difference does it make?" said Garret. "So long's we

get some whales. For every whale we take, it's money in our pockets. No whales, no money."

"Then there are whales there?" I asked.

The men chuckled, shaking their heads.

Irish grinned. "What did you expect, laddie? Mermaids?"

The older sailor said, "Couple of years ago, some lucky fellow discovered thousands of whales in the Arctic, swimming round happy as ye please. Polar whales, they be called. Great fat things. Friend of mine said one whale makes two hundred barrels of oil."

"Ah, shut yer gob," said Irish. "No whale makes that much."

"Who be ye telling to shut his gob?"

I wasn't much interested in the boxing match that followed. I ignored the wagers, the cries of encouragement, the laughter. I got up and walked to the rail. Below, the water rushed by with a gurgle. To the west, the sky was still light; to the east, black, stars appearing by the hundreds. From the stern of the ship, I heard the tinkling of a piano and a woman's voice singing, *"Now speed ye on, my gallant bark, our hopes are all in thee; Swift bear us to our peaceful home, far o'er the deep blue sea. . . ."*

And then Dexter was beside me.

"The Arctic?" I asked, turning to him. "Why didn't you ask all the proper questions when we signed?"

"Well, it's certain *you* didn't. All you cared about was bugs." Dexter leaned against the rail, smiled, and shrugged. "Doesn't matter. I mean, how bad can it be?"

"There she blo-o-o-ows!"

The cry pealed through the morning air and shivered down the mast, into every timber and every heart. In the fo'c'sle, men stopped shoveling food into their mouths and stared at each other. For a split second, no one moved or breathed.

"There she blo-o-o-ows!"

Then everyone went right crazy. I spilled my coffee down my dungarees. Dexter's plum duff plopped onto the floor, along with his tin dish. Irish cursed as he stubbed his toe against his sea chest and tumbled headlong into his bunk, ripping his calico curtain. The companionway jammed with men. I don't even remember hustling up the companionway, but suddenly I was on deck, running aft toward the starboard quarter boat, my heart racing as if I were a hound after a rabbit.

"Luff up to the wind!" cried the captain.

"Aye, aye, sir!"

"There she blo-o-o-ows! A whole school of them, sir!"

"How far away?"

"A half mile, sir!"

"Blood and thunder! Practically ran over them. Hard down the wheel! Haul aback the mainyard! Fetch me some whales, boys!"

To the rattle of blocks, we lowered our boat with the fourth mate and the harponeer, Adam Briggs, aboard. Then, just as we'd practiced many times, Garret, Dexter, Irish, and I slid down the falls and into the boat.

Following orders, we quickly set our sail and began to paddle. The breeze caught us and we sped downwind toward the whales. In the stern of the whaleboat, the fourth mate, Henry Sweet, whispered, "Don't be afeard now, boys. Just remember your duties and think of all that oil. We'll bathe in it tonight, so bend your backs to them paddles. Quiet now, me hearties. Don't gally the whales. They don't know what's a-coming. Sweet Mother of God, our wives and daughters and sisters depend on us. . . ."

We were just south of the equator, and though the morning was young and breezy, sweat streamed from me. Round about I heard the sounds of heavy breathing. I smelled sweat, damp dungarees, wet wood. The four boats were neck and neck, ours closest to the whales by half a boat length. Dip, dip, dip went the paddles.

Then, up ahead, I heard it. The hollow sound of a sperm whale releasing its air. A giant, moist bellows. *Blood and thunder.* While I now knew that sperm whales really didn't eat people, that Father had spun me a yarn sure to scare me to the devil, still . . .

I glanced at Dexter. His eyes were as big as twenty-dollar gold coins. It was the moment we'd waited for all these years.

Closer . . . closer . . . I saw them now—saw their black backs; slick, great forms beneath the water. . . .

The whaleboat glided silently, the wind barely a whisper in her sail.

I stared into the seething water ahead, my heart banging like a brass drum. *Holy angels in heaven.* Was that an eye? Were those teeth?

"Faster, boys," whispered Sweet. "Give me all ye've got."

Then it happened. I accidentally hit the side of the boat with my paddle. *Ka-thunk!* I froze as the sound echoed through the water like a rifle shot. Immediately, the whales sank out of sight, leaving only bubbles and an oily slick behind. My face flushed hotter than Hades. *Blast it all! I've ruined our first hunt!*

Sure enough, the first mate stood in his boat and hollered, "They're gallying to windward! The whole lot of them! Take down the mast, stow your blasted paddles, put your oars to the locks, boys, and pull!" Next he let loose with a string of rip-roaring curses, screaming, with my name mixed up in all of it.

I'd never before heard such salty language. From the mates, the harponeers, my shipmates—coming at me from every side. Even Dexter cast me an irritated glance. What had been an easy sail downwind toward unsuspecting whales was now a hard pull to windward. I said nothing. Instead, I faced the stern, where the fourth mate stood scowling, his black eyebrows scrunched together, and put my body to the oar.

Puffing and pulling, groaning at the oars, we passed the *Sea Hawk*. Even from a distance, I heard the curses Captain Thorndike shouted at me. The shipkeepers—the cooper, the cook, the carpenter, the steward, and the ship's boy—shouted curses. If I hadn't already known I was stupid, a dullard and a dunce and an idiot, good for nothing but fish food, I knew it now. I prayed that Elizabeth Thorndike didn't know my name, didn't know it was me who was the stupid greenie.

Suddenly, I longed for home, for Aunt Agatha, wishing I'd never heard of the *Sea Hawk*.

Only a whale can save me now.

"The signals on the masthead say the school is three miles to windward," said Sweet. "Oh, jolly day. Pull, boys, pull. Break your backs a-pulling. Bones, ye let it happen again and I'll split your head open and have your brains for supper."

"Och!" exclaimed Irish. "It'd make for a wee meal. Hardly worth dirtying a fork."

"Who said I was going to use a fork?"

"Aw, leave him alone," said Garret, grunting as he talked. "It's his first hunt. Most everyone fouls up their first hunt, I reckon."

"Did you?" asked Dexter.

"Well, no," Garret replied, "but that don't mean nothing."

"Don't you worry none, Bones," Garret said every now and then between pulls. "Plenty of men have done the same."

"Thanks," I mumbled.

For four hours we pulled, the conversation eventually dwindling to grunts and an occasional whispered oath. My oar was sticky with blood. My hands screamed with every pull. My back ached. My lungs burned. The sun blazed, and I tasted sweat. I'd never imagined whaling to be such terrible hard work.

By now the other three whaleboats were strewn out to either side of us, perhaps a half mile separating the two farthest boats. For the longest time I heard nothing but the quiet slap of the oars, the tinkle of water, the creak of the oarlocks, the breathing of my shipmates.

I peered into the water. Seemed bottomless, it did, murky and frightening. Just then, a horrible thought occurred to me. *Is this where Father died?*

Suddenly, I saw a shadowy shape beneath me. I blinked. My heart lurched. *Could it be . . . Was it . . .*

The water became darker, black almost, and I knew from the surge in my blood it was a whale rising. *Close, too close!* Before I could cry out, the whale erupted from the water with a blast from his blowhole. A mist stung me, a stench of rot, as the whale's body blotted out the sun, his vast form suspended in the air.

A monster.

Big as a building.

CHAPTER
4

"Mother of mercy!" cried Irish.

The monster's jaw snapped, and I saw the glistening of teeth.

In the same moment, the harponeer stood and cast his iron deep into the whale's hide. "Stern all! Stern for your lives!" Briggs screamed as he grabbed his second iron and darted it into the whale as well.

I rowed for my very life. *God help us! We'll capsize!*

With a crack like thunder, the whale crashed into the water. A wave like the tide roared over us. The whaleboat rolled onto her side, and for a desperate moment I clung to the gunwale, choking on seawater. Then the boat righted herself, half filled with water.

"Stern all!" yelled Sweet. "Before he smashes us with his flukes!"

Dexter began to bail, as that was his job. With the others I found my seat and rowed like the dickens. Suddenly, with a shriek, the whaleline flew past my shoulder as the injured whale sped to windward.

"Avast!" cried Sweet. "We're in for a ride! Bail, boys, bail! All of ye!"

I bailed like a crazy man as the line whistled hot and sizzling round the loggerhead in the stern, forward the length of the boat, and out the bow's chocks. Smoke rose from the loggerhead. The air stank of burning hemp. The bow dipped low. Terrible low. I'd heard yarns of how if the line caught in the chocks, it yanked the boat under in an instant, men and all, never to be seen again. *Blood and thunder!* I'd heard tales of men getting caught in the line as it whizzed out of the tubs, a coil wrapped round an arm, an ankle, the poor fellows whipping right out of the whaleboat and down into the deep so fast no one saw them go. *By fire!*

Then, with a groan and a shudder, our whaleboat took off, dashing along, the line stretched taut between us and the whale. I clung to my seat, tasting blood, teeth jarring together, as we crashed from one wave to the next, rocking back and forth, blinded by spray. *Jerusalem crickets! Is every chase like this?*

In the midst of all this dashing along, Briggs and Sweet exchanged places, stem to stern. They staggered with the motion of the whaleboat, a hand on this shoulder, a hand on that head to steady themselves. Half covered my eyes, Briggs did. About broke my neck with his weight. Briggs would now steer the boat, while Sweet would make the kill. It was tradition.

Finally, the whale began to slow. With two irons in him already, he was tiring.

"Haul in! Haul in!" cried Sweet from the bow.

We grabbed the line and pulled hand over fist. Inch by inch, foot by foot, gaining back every thread of rope the whale had taken. Hundreds of feet, it seemed. My muscles screamed. I left blood on the line. Then, finally, our boat thumped against the whale's back. Wood to blackskin, as they say.

Sweet went to work with his lance. Monster or not, it was gruesome. I gripped the gunwale, sweating, nauseated, as man and beast struggled. Seemed forever.

Then, with a final bloody blast from its spout, showering us with gore, the creature stopped thrashing. The foamy water settled and all became still.

"It's dead," said Sweet, wiping blood from his eyes.

Everything, every one of us was soaked crimson. Like murderers, we looked. The blood was hot and horrible and I wanted to cry.

Whaling was nothing like I'd imagined.

I sat forward on the windlass, eating, shaking with exhaustion. *What a day.*

Dexter shoveled food into his mouth with his knife and fingers. His palms were raw, crusty with blood, his wrists swollen. Garret sat on my other side, but he was turned away, telling everyone for the fourth or fifth time how the whale had blasted out of the water, how it had swamped our boat, and such. Aye, it made for good telling, but I was full of it.

As the sun began to dip beneath the horizon, the waters aglow, a shadow fell across me. I looked up, my mouth full of doughboy. 'Twas Captain Thorndike. I stopped midchew. He was outlined with sunset, cast in shadow, smoke from his pipe wisping round him. The pipe looked like a child's toy in his giant hand. Garret and Dexter stopped eating too. All round me it seemed everyone held his breath, and what had been a ship filled with noise was now dreadful silent. I swallowed my doughboy with a gulp.

"Nicholas Robbins?"

"Aye, sir."

Thorndike took a puff from his pipe. The tobacco glowed orange. The smell pinched my nose. "I've no mind to put up with sloppy work and greenies who don't know their job. Ye were careless, and it cost us a day's work and 'most cost us a whale."

I looked down. Studied my feet.

The pipe hissed as Thorndike took another puff. Above me a sail flapped. Then the captain brought his face level with mine. I shrank back. His voice was calm yet threatening, as if a storm brewed inside him. A monstrous storm. "Let it happen again, boy, and I'll yank your arms from their sockets. Aye, that I will." He blew smoke in my face and straightened to face everyone. "Now, normally I would be of a mind to give everyone a night's rest and start cutting in the whale in the morning. But we've lost a whole day, and I've no mind for rewarding carelessness. Finish your supper and get to work, boys. There'll be no rest till it's done."

As Thorndike strolled aft, I stared at my plate, my appetite blown away like tobacco smoke, feeling everyone stare at me. *If my shipmates didn't hate me before,* I thought, *they hate me now. Blast it, I should never have come.* For the millionth time that day, hot tears pressed against my eyelids.

Then, just when I thought things couldn't get any worse, another shadow blocked the sinking sun. "Why, if I didn't know better, I'd say Bones be crying."

I tensed.

It was Adam Briggs, our harponeer. He was broad-shouldered, pimple-faced, about twenty years old. I didn't like him much—he seemed arrogant and big-mouthed, even if he could toss an iron within an inch of a target. I wished he would just shrivel up and blow away. I looked up, wanting to tell him that, but the three other harponeers stood behind Briggs, arms crossed, and I thought I might get my face smashed.

Beside me, Dexter said, "It was a simple mistake. Could have happened to any of us."

"But it didn't." Briggs stepped closer.

"Aw," said Garret. "Leave him alone. I reckon anyone's a mite scared on his first hunt. And like Dexter said, he didn't mean nothing by it."

"Shut up, Carrot Sticks. Besides, anyone with eyeballs could tell that Nick here wasn't *a mite* scared. He was a sniveling baby. Most yellow-livered coward I ever saw. What about it, boys?" He glanced over his shoulder as the other harponeers nodded and grunted and echoed, "Sniveling baby" and "Yellow-livered coward."

"I'm sorry," I mumbled. "Sorry I hit the boat with my paddle. Sorry I ever came along."

"There. Satisfied?" said Dexter. "He said he was sorry. Now why don't you fellows go along and leave us be?"

Just then, Briggs shoved my plate into my face. Beans, rice, and doughboys smeared my cheeks. Rice plopped from my eyelashes. I stared stupidly, wondering what to do. Should I fight? Should I ignore him? Should I beat it to the fo'c'sle? But before I could do anything, Dexter tossed his plate aside and jumped to his feet. He waved his fists in front of Briggs' face. "You touch him again and I'll bust you!"

"Dexter, no!" I cried.

But I was too late. Briggs wound up and punched Dexter in the gut. In a flash they were on the deck, fists and curses flying, going at it hammer and tongs. I launched myself on top of Briggs, trying to pull him off of Dexter, screaming something, I don't know what. Garret was in there too, red hair flashing in the sunset. Someone boxed my jaw. I fell flat and saw stars.

Then, almost as soon as it had begun, it was over. The mates kicked us apart and yanked to our feet those of us who were flat out. My chest heaved and I still saw stars. Then Captain Thorndike was there, bellowing, demanding to know what had happened. Everyone talked at once. Accusations flew. I swayed on my feet, trying not to fall over.

Suddenly, there was silence. That terrible silence I was learning to hate so much.

"Trice Dexter Robbins thumbs up to the rigging," thundered Thorndike, his voice splintering the stillness. "I'll not have a greenie making trouble aboard my ship. I warned all of ye that there'd be no fighting aboard the *Sea Hawk*. And if ye can't abide the rules, ye must abide the consequences. As for Briggs, send him to the fo'c'sle as a regular hand—"

"The fo'c'sle!" exploded Briggs. "You can't demote me! I'm the one who—"

Captain Thorndike's giant fist slammed into Briggs' face. I heard the crunch of bone. Blood spurted. Briggs dropped to his knees and gave a strangled cry. A gurgle. He gasped. "Ye broke my nose! Ye broke my nose!"

Thorndike watched Briggs awhile, saying nothing. Then, without moving, he barked, "Garret Hix!"

Garret's eyes flew open wide. "Aye, sir!"

"You're the new harponeer for your boat. Do ye think you're up for the task?"

"Aye, sir!"

"Move your things to steerage. And as for the rest of ye," screamed Thorndike, his scar purple as a bruise, "get to work before I trice all of ye!"

Trice.

I hadn't known what it meant before.

They tied a rope round each of Dexter's thumbs and hoisted him until his toes just skimmed the deck. As the *Sea Hawk* rocked to starboard, he could no longer touch the deck and hung by his thumbs alone. Pain flashed across his face like a cloud passing the sun. He hung motionless, silent, toes scraping back and forth with the movement of the ship.

After a time, I left the windlass, where I'd been put to work. *By fire, I'm a man, aren't I? And men don't leave their brothers triced by their thumbs in the rigging!* I found Captain Thorndike looking over the ship's gangway, where the mates were cutting in the whale. Sharks snapped and the water frothed with blood. The *Sea Hawk* heeled to starboard, quivering and groaning with the weight of the whale's blubber.

The captain had his back to me.

"Captain Thorndike—"

"Return to your station, sailor."

I bit my lip while my heart went off to the races. "But—but Captain Thorndike—"

He turned, eyes narrowed. "Obey me, sailor, before I make ye sorry."

My stomach flipped. I wanted to dash back to the windlass. "It was all my fault. Dexter was protecting me. You see, we're brothers. He shouldn't be—"

Suddenly, the captain grabbed my shirtfront and slammed me into the bulwarks. I winced as my ribs crunched against the wood. *What the—* Thorndike lowered his face into mine. Garret had told me that the captain had been chewed in the mouth of a sperm whale and then spat out because he tasted so bad, and that's how he got his scar. Near tore his head in half. I didn't believe it then, but I believed it now. His scar throbbed. His eyes bulged. I smelled his supper. "Captain, sir, please—"

"Say one more word, Robbins, and not only will I trice ye by your thumbs alongside your brother, but your brother will hang an hour longer, aye, that he will. Now I have one thing to say to ye, and one thing only. Ye be a sorry excuse for a whaleman. Ye be no more than a blubbering girl that needs her hand held and her nose wiped. Either learn your job and learn it fast or I'll toss ye overboard as a waste of grub. Now get out of my sight. Ye make me sick to look at ye."

He flung me away and I stumbled to my knees.

Then, to my horror, I saw Elizabeth standing by the steerage companionway, watching, handkerchief over her nose and mouth, her face drained of color. *Why, she heard everything Thorndike said to me!* As the familiar heat blazed in my cheeks, I stumbled to the windlass and put my back to the work. My teeth ached from clenching my jaw. *By fire, I hate that man. I hate Thorndike. I hate the* Sea Hawk. *I hate whaling. I wish I'd never come.*

CHAPTER 5

*F*inally, long after night had fallen and under the light of a few dim, soot-coated lanterns, Thorndike lowered Dexter to the deck.

He took a wobbly step and then, with a look of defiance, threw his head back and swaggered toward us as if nothing were the matter and he'd merely been hoisted for some fresh air. His thumbs told the tale, though. They were swollen and reddish purple, marked deep with hemp burn.

"A brave lad," said Irish as he approached. "Got guts of iron, so he does." Dexter said nothing, just put his weight to the windlass bar, and to the cry of "Heave pawl!" started back to work. Heavy chains clanked on the deck, iron pawls rattled, and the windlass groaned.

After the blubber was aboard, and after

the crew hurrahed and cried, "Five and forty more!" the trypot fires were lit and the carcass released, already covered with screaming birds. Earlier, the whale's head had been severed from the body, and now it was lashed to the gangway. In the dim lantern light, it looked eerie, a ghost of a whale.

"You, Bones." Cole, the first mate, pointed at me. "Strip naked and climb in. You're skinny. You'll fit like a stick in a barrel."

"What?" I gaped at him. *Is he joking? Strip naked? Climb in? Into what? The head?*

All round me I saw men nudging each other with their elbows, grinning, as if to say, *Look at the yellow-livered coward. Won't climb into a whale's head.*

The second mate, whose name was Samuel Walker, laughed. "Stupid greenie, what do ye think we're going to do? Sew ye up inside and drop ye into the ocean? Besides, ye won't be doing it alone."

Horrified, I saw Garret stripping naked beside me. I mean *naked. God almighty.* With a sympathetic glance at me, Garret slipped and slid onto the head and down into a hole that had been cut. His head poked out.

Climb? In there? Naked as the day I was born? In front of everyone?

An awful flush started at the base of my neck and burst upward to the roots of my hair. Aunt Agatha always said I was the fastest flusher this side of the Mississippi. I glanced around furiously, wondering how I could get out of this. But when I saw clouds gathering on Cole's face, I knew I had about two seconds to follow orders or else.

"Ah, Jeez."

I tore off my clothes, every last stitch, and climbed onto the head, praying Elizabeth wasn't watching from somewheres. I felt myself blaze with embarrassment and heard laughter and guffaws. Taking a quick breath, I lowered myself inside. *Blood and thunder. It's squishy and disgusting. Hot. Soupy.* Liquid-filled cells were everywhere, like a giant honeycomb.

"You see, Bones," said Garret as he dipped a bucket into the head, talking casual, as if we were on a picnic, as if everyone weren't standing there laughing at me, "a sperm whale's head is like a camel's hump. Ain't no other way to explain it, really. Oil is stored in the head like water's stored in a hump." He clapped me on the back. "Aw, c'mon. Don't look so blamed pop-eyed. It's what puts money in your pocket."

"Right now I don't have any pockets."

Cole handed me a bucket. "Stopper your tonsils and get to work, Bones. We don't run a nursery here."

For the next hour or so, surrounded by slurping and sucking sounds, Garret and I hacked and scooped with knives and buckets, emptying out the head. The white liquid congealed as it came in contact with the air, like hot wax suddenly cooled. We were covered with pulp, ooze, slime. Finally finished, Garret and I slipped out of the head, rinsed, and dressed. My skin was soft, as though I'd bathed in lotion.

Meanwhile, others poured the oily liquid into the trypots to boil. Once it was boiled and put into casks, slabs of blubber were hauled up from the blubber room, minced, and piled into the trypots to melt into oil. As the blubber melted, the shriveled skins and solids were skimmed out of the trypots and thrown into the fire as fuel. The fire hissed and flared with a roaring gasp, belching out of the double chimney and into the night. The sails flickered orange. Embers spat upward. We looked like hell afloat.

For most of the night, I was screamed at—curses mixed with "stupid blasted greenie," followed by a kick or two on the backside. Cole swung a marlinspike at my head, but I ducked and hurried away. He said it was the fastest he'd ever seen me move. Fact was, I didn't know what to do unless someone *was* screaming at me, telling me where to go and what to do. I'd never boiled a whale before.

The scuppers were stoppered so that none of the oil could leak overboard. Dungarees rolled up to my knees, sockless, I waded through blood, oil, and seawater, my brogans squashing with every step as slime squished between my toes. Boiling whale smelled about as nice as a dead pig buried in rotted cheese.

Toward morning, I slipped in the slop and landed flat on my back. I lay there a moment out of everyone's way just to catch my breath. It was my first rest since the morning before. *Did Father ever work this hard? Did Father ever swing a marlinspike at anyone's head? Smash anyone's nose? Am I really a blubbering girl?*

"Here." Dexter held out a hand to help me up. His face was black and shiny from greasy soot, his eyes reddened from smoke.

I staggered to my feet. "You look like the devil."

"Aye." He grinned, his teeth startling white against the black. "So do you."

I glanced at his hands. "You all right?"

"Nothing a little whale oil won't cure."

"Sorry I got you into a scrape."

He shrugged, but I could tell he wasn't happy with me. I'd let him down, likely, just as I'd let down everybody else. "They're cooking doughnuts in the trypots. Go get you some before it's too late."

"No." I shook my head, my throat tightening. "Don't feel so good right now."

Dexter nodded. Most times, it wasn't necessary to explain things to him. He always seemed to know anyways. "You hated it, didn't you?" I knew he was talking about the hunt.

"Aye." My voice thickened. "Thorndike says I'm a sorry excuse for a whaleman. That I'm a blubbering girl. And now everybody thinks I'm—I'm a coward."

I was hoping he would argue with me, tell me I was a right excellent whaleman and brave as Caesar, but he didn't. "You always were too soft-hearted."

"So what should I do?"

At that moment, my heart tumbled, for Thorndike approached, glowering, looking like the devil of devils. I left Dexter and hurried back to work, weak with relief when Thorndike faded back into the shadows.

On New Year's Day, just over two months out of New Bedford, I got myself brained.

I was climbing the ratlines to furl the main topgallant and royal when Briggs muscled past, at the same time planting a sharp elbow on my temple. "Out of my way, idiot!" I lost my footing, slipped sideways off the shrouds and dangled above the deck, feet kicking, before my fingers gave way and I fell. It wasn't a long fall, but it was hard. My teeth slammed together and I bit off a piece of my tongue. I lay there wondering where I was and why I was flat on my back and why Briggs looked so ugly whenever he grinned.

"Get up." First Mate Cole stood over me, glowering. The wind was gathering force, for we were headed west round Cape Horn, into some of the most treacherous waters known to mariners. It was raining, a freezing, stinging rain, and icebergs floated round. All hands had been ordered aloft to shorten sail. "I said, get up!"

He kicked me when I didn't move. It was a sharp kick, aimed at my ribs. I gasped with pain. When I still didn't move, couldn't, he put on his brass knuckles and went to work on me. Garret told me later that Cole beat me for two minutes straight. That Dexter and Garret and Irish had to pull him off me, that Dexter had to call for help but not before Cole had broken four of my ribs and my nose and beaten the rest of my face to a bloody pulp. When questioned by the captain, Cole swore I'd disobeyed a direct order. That old ladies with broken legs moved faster than I did. Thorndike nodded, said I was a sorry excuse for a whaleman, the most inept sailor he'd ever known, and that maybe this would knock some nautical sense into me. I was put on the sick list.

I don't remember much about being brained, only that I lay in my bunk day after day, hating Thorndike, hating the *Sea Hawk,* hating Briggs' pimply, arrogant face, adding Cole to my hate list, my face throbbing, every breath afire, my tongue sore, my nose swollen and blood-filled, while storms raged round me and I thought we would all sink and drown.

At first, Dexter visited me after his watches ended, sometimes bringing me broth and coffee and hard bread. But after a while he just crawled into the bunk above me without changing his clothes. He shivered before falling asleep as the ship reeled and shrieked and a heavy head sea pounded the bow again and again like a giant fist.

One night, Briggs woke me from a deep sleep. "Hey, Bones," he whispered in my ear. "There be a fat rat a-chewing on your toenails."

Slowly, I rolled over, away from his arrogant whisper. *Go away. I hate you.* My corn-husk mattress crunched beneath me. Pain was flashing through my ribs when, by fire, I *did* feel something furry down by my feet. My eyes popped open. I peered at my feet. A huge rat sat on his haunches, helping himself to my toenails.

I shrieked, high and girl-like, at the same time flailing like an idiot. I slammed my head on the upper bunk.

Briggs roared with laughter.

And while I struggled to get out of my bunk, Briggs tossed a handful of cockroaches at me. They landed in my face. My hair. Again I shrieked, pawing at myself.

41

The fo'c'sle was in an uproar. Men who'd been asleep awakened, sitting upright with alarm. Those who'd been watching roared alongside Briggs. And through it all I shrieked, finally flinging myself from my bunk. I stood in the middle of the fo'c'sle now, shaking, half crying, blood pounding in my ears and dribbling out my nose. Pain throbbed through my ribs so bad I clutched my sides, groaned, and sank to my knees.

Cockroaches swarmed over my bedding. The rat was nowhere to be seen.

Dexter had been sleeping, but now he looked at me, his hair frazzled. I reckon it didn't take a whale-oil expert to figure what had happened, what with Briggs roaring with laughter. Dexter climbed out of his bunk and, without saying a word, began tossing the cockroaches out one by one and hammering them with his brogan. He shook out my blankets, checked all sides of my mattress and every corner of my bunk.

"Awww, ain't that so sweet," said Briggs as Dexter helped me back into bed.

Dexter covered me, wiped my nose with a hanky, and whispered, "I've been thinking."

"What do you mean?"

Dexter glanced round to see if anyone was listening, but the fo'c'sle was still in chaos, men yakking or laughing or hollering for everyone to shut the hell up. "I've been thinking of leaving."

I blinked. "Leaving? You mean deserting?"

"Shh. Aye."

"Why?"

He sighed. "Look at yourself, Nick. You're a blasted mess."

I groaned. "Have you seen yourself lately?" Dark shadows were stamped below Dexter's eyes. His hair stuck out every which way.

"Aye. I've a boil on my neck that's near killing me. I lost a fingernail today somewheres up on the mainmast. Most times I'm so cold I can't feel my hands or feet when I'm aloft."

"But what about your dreams?"

He shrugged. "Aunt Agatha made me swear on our mother's grave that I'd bring you home in one piece. Face it, Nick, whaling isn't for you. Some men love it. Some men hate it. When we stop to reprovision at the Sandwich Islands, we'll desert. I'll go whaling again once we're home."

"You're a true brother, Dex."

Dexter ran a hand through his hair and sighed. "So what about it?"

I nodded, blinking back tears. "I want to go home."

The next day, Briggs was snoring away in his bunk.

Dexter crept up and, slick as you please, dumped a pint of dried peas into Briggs' open mouth. As Briggs exploded upward, midsnore, choking, Dexter sprinted across the fo'c'sle and sprang into his bunk quick as an antelope. We all pretended not to notice, of course. We pretended to be sleeping, or picking our nails, or writing a letter, as Briggs gagged and spluttered and cursed and told everyone he was going to kill whoever had done it.

"Ah, now, Briggs," said Irish finally, "you got to admit it was no more than you deserved."

"Shut your face, Irish."

"Bad day, is it you're having?"

"I almost choked to death!"

"What a pity," drawled Dexter. "Why don't you go tell the captain? He'll wipe your tears with his fist."

Just then, the wind shrieked and the ship heeled sharply. Briggs crashed against his bunk. Boots and clothing slid across the fo'c'sle floor. Feet hammered the deck overhead as someone hollered down the companionway, "All hands! All hands to shorten sail!"

Men tumbled out of their bunks and pelted for the ladder, scrambling to don their boots and oilskins as they cursed and ran.

Moving quickly, Briggs scraped up the peas and plunked them into his tin pint pot. After stowing them, he put on his oilskins, snugged on his sou'wester, and said to me, "What're you staring at? Finders keepers. They're mine now." And out he went.

CHAPTER
6

*B*esides seeing dried peas poured down Briggs' throat, there were two good things about being on the sick list, stuck in the fo'c'sle for three weeks straight.

First, I began to carve whale teeth like my father used to. Scrimshaw, it was called, and I believe I was right good at it. Fact was, Irish peeped into my bunk to see how I was feeling, and when he saw the tooth I was carving, he whistled and told everyone to come have a look. Everyone straggled out of their bunks, excepting Briggs, of course, and admired my carving. It was of an eagle snagging a fish from the water, struggling to lift its prey. Right then and there the boys bid for my tooth. It sold to Irish for two doughboys, one plum duff, and a new pair of wool socks straight from the slop chest. I was proud. "Never knew you had it in you," said Dexter.

The second good thing about being on the sick list was that Elizabeth came to see me. Well, her mother came too. And not just to see me, but to see all the fellows who were sick or hurt. And there were plenty.

On that day the door banged open. Wind gusted through the fo'c'sle. The lanterns flared and I smelled a faint scent of perfume. Lilacs, maybe. Armed with bandages, iodine, scissors, and such-like, Mrs. Thorndike and Elizabeth climbed down the companion-way. Duff, the steward, followed and began pouring coffee for everyone, slopping more onto the floor than into the cups. It was eight bells and the change of watches, so the women first tended one watch, then another, while the door opened and closed, men going in and out dressed in their oilskins and sou'westers.

At first, Elizabeth looked scared, as if she'd never been in the fo'c'sle before. Certain it must have looked wretched, what with clothes piled knee deep, coats moldering on pegs, cockroaches and rats, men groaning in their bunks, and a stink that would shrivel a dog. Nose and fingers pink with cold, slender like her mother, with high cheekbones, Elizabeth dabbed the moisture off her face with a lace-trimmed hanky. I swear I could see the entire ocean in her eyes.

Tucking her hanky down the wrist of her sleeve, Elizabeth saw me and smiled. I felt color creeping past my collar, remembering the last time she'd seen me—getting chewed out by her father for being a poor excuse of a whaleman. When she looked away, I licked my hands and smoothed my hair back and scrubbed my face as best I could. It wouldn't do to look as if I'd been wallowing in a pigpen during a hurricane.

"Elizabeth, pay attention," said her mother, yanking her arm. "A good captain's daughter will someday make a good captain's wife. These are duties to which ye must attend." So saying, Mrs. Thorndike leaned over Irish's wrist and made a quick incision on a boil. Irish paled as blood and pus drained into a bowl. Mrs. Thorndike cleaned the boil with iodine and wrapped it in bandages, all the while explaining to Elizabeth what she was doing. "'Tis the chafing of the wet oilskins that causes the boils. . . . And of course, this be frostbite. Cape Horn fever, we call it."

They made their way round all the bunks, finally stopping at Dexter's bunk above me. Mrs. Thorndike was talking to Dexter, asking him how he was feeling, when Elizabeth leaned down to me and whispered, "You're staring."

I flushed, suddenly finding the underside of the upper bunk most interesting.

"What's your name?" she whispered.

But before I could answer, Mrs. Thorndike yanked Elizabeth upright. "Pay attention, young lady. This poor sailor's telling us all about his boils and all ye can do is lollygag. Time's a-wasting."

"Yes, Mother."

"Now I want you to lance his boils, clean them, and bandage them just like I shown you."

"Yes, Mother."

Soon it was my turn.

"Why, young man, it doesn't look as if you've set foot out of your quarters for days."

"Uh—yes'm."

"What's ailing you, then?"

"I—uh—fell out of the rigging."

"Funny, I didn't hear of it. Usually Mr. Thorndike informs me of such occasions."

"He must've forgotten."

She asked me what I'd hurt in my fall, and I told her, aware that Elizabeth was watching and listening. After my explanation,

Mrs. Thorndike began examining me. She was a stern-looking woman, narrow-faced, her faded yellow hair pulled back tightly. Tiny wrinkles played at the corners of her eyes. She looked to be in her mid-forties.

I winced when she examined my ribs.

"Does it still hurt?"

"Yes'm."

"Take another week of rest, and then report for light duty."

"Yes'm."

"Well, Elizabeth, we've done our duty for today. Gather our things together, and mind ye hold on to the lifeline."

Elizabeth flashed a smile at me before following her mother out of the fo'c'sle.

There was a brief silence after they left before Irish said, "Well now, Bones, I think the lass has taken a fancy to the cut of your jib, though why is a mystery!"

"Must be the dashing air about him," said another sailor; "you know, his elegance and ease."

"Must be all them muscles."

"Couldn't be his brains."

"Maybe she's just a wee bit seasick."

"She'd have to be."

"Poor lass."

"Ah, don't worry none. Ol' lover-boy Nick will cheer her right up. Ain't that right, Bones?"

I didn't answer, grinning so hard my cheeks ached. *By fire, I think I'm cured.*

"Good girl, that's my good girl." I patted Ninny's side as she nibbled my sleeve. Then, after rubbing my hands together, I began to milk the goat. "I know, girl, you miss your baby and my hands are cold, but hold still now. Eat your grain and let me do my job."

Goat duty.

That's what everyone called it. The cook, the steward, everyone thought it was a tedious chore, but I loved it. Besides being a fine producer, giving upwards of a gallon a day, Ninny was a good goat. Friendly and sweet. From the time I first scratched behind her ears, behind her little horns, she bleated for me whenever I passed, straining against the rope round her neck. It was the beginning of February, and ever since being taken off the sick list the week before (not long after Ninny had given birth to a kid that ended up adorning the captain's table), I'd been given permanent goat duty. And though we were headed north now, toward the equator and the Sandwich Islands, it was still nippy.

"Almost done, girl. Steady there."

Someone giggled beside me. "Do you always talk to animals?"

Startled, I felt heat blaze up my neck. "I didn't know anyone was listening."

Elizabeth laughed again and moved closer, the orange tabby nestled in her arms. Her waist-length hair was tied back in a blue ribbon that matched her eyes and her bonnet. A faint scent of lilac caught the breeze. "What do they call you besides Bones?"

I glanced round quickly. "Who, me?"

"Of course you, silly."

"Nick—I mean, Nicholas Robbins." I glanced round again, knowing that if anyone caught me talking to Miss Elizabeth, I was dead. Even though I liked her fine, I wished she'd go away.

"Well, hello, then." She breathed deeply, looking about. "Why, it's a right fine day, Mr. Robbins. Don't you think?"

"Uh—well—aye."

I milked awhile in silence, trying to think of something to say. But all I could think of was how the old man was going to kill me. Trice? Hanging? Maybe he would just fling me overboard as a waste of grub. No need for a burial. "Uh—Miss Elizabeth, if anyone catches me talking to you, why, the old man—I mean—you know, Captain Thorn—" I choked on my words, for she plunked herself on the deck beside me, arranging her skirts as if she were sitting for a picnic, placing her cat on her lap.

Oh, dear sweet holy angels in heaven. I'm in trouble now.

The cat meowed and Elizabeth rubbed its head.

"What's its name?" I asked, unable to think of anything smarter to say.

"Prince Albert. I found him by the waterfront a week before we set sail. He was lost and hungry." She stroked the cat and I heard it purr. "Gets awful lonesome in the cabin by myself, you know. I'm not allowed to talk to anyone except Cook and Duff. My parents, well, they watch my every move as if I was going to do something horrid. Stand in the sun without a bonnet or climb the mainmast dressed in nothing but my petticoats or something equally silly."

"Oh." I kept glancing round to see if we were being watched. My neck prickled as I imagined Thorndike grabbing me from behind and shaking me like a dog shakes a rat.

"Of course, Mother and Father had a fit when I brought the cat aboard. They have a fit about everything. Said the best thing for it was the dinner table." Seeing the expression on my face, she laughed. "Oh, Nick—can I call you that?—I'm only kidding! No, they let me keep it, but only if it doesn't make any noise or pester them." She was silent, hugging the cat, seeming lost in thought. Then she said, "You're different from the rest of them."

I milked faster. "How so?"

"I don't know. It's just that you—you seem so . . . nice."

Nice? Being nice was about as exciting as a wart. I wanted to appear rugged and strong and as brave as Dexter.

"Oh, don't look so disappointed! Nice is good!"

When I said nothing, she said, "In fact, you remind me of my brother."

"Your brother?" I hadn't recalled seeing a boy around.

"Aye. You look just like Thomas. It was the first thing I noticed when I saw you."

"Where is he?"

She shrugged. "He was lost at sea a couple years ago. Father said he was the finest whaleman he'd ever seen and would have made a fine captain. He was already second mate."

"Oh, sorry," I said, meanwhile thinking, *Terrific! I look like Thorndike's dead son. Me—a pathetic excuse for a whaleman and a blubbering girl besides.* "I—I really shouldn't be talking to you, Miss Elizabeth. I could get into a heap of trouble, you know."

Her eyes brightened and she grinned impishly. "But you're not talking, I am."

Ninny bleated and nibbled my hair. I couldn't help smiling and scratching her side. "All done now. You're a good girl, Ninny."

"See? That's what I mean. How many men would pat a goat and tell her she's a good girl?"

I was stumped. "How many?"

She covered her mouth with her hand and laughed again.

I felt my face flush bright as a tomato, realizing I'd just made a perfect fool of myself. Again. "I—I'd better go, Miss Elizabeth. Sorry about your brother." I grabbed the milk bucket, but before I could dash away like the idiot I was, she put her hand on my arm.

"Please don't change. Don't become like everybody else. Please." Her blue eyes were clear, sad somehow. "And I'm sorry about what Father said to you the other day. He's like that sometimes. I think you bring out the worst in him."

"Why?" I couldn't help asking.

She shrugged. "I don't know. I—I guess because you're not my brother and never will be."

I tried to swallow, my mouth dry as sand. "Bye," I croaked, slopping milk out of the bucket as I stumbled toward the galley, remembering the old man's words, *Ye make me sick to look at ye.*

I told Dexter about my looking like Thorndike's dead son. Lying on his bunk, chest bare, Dexter was quiet for a moment, running a hand through his hair. "Of all the blasted luck," he finally whispered. "Wouldn't you rather have put up with a few bugs?"

"You're the one who was drooling, saying she was the ship of your dreams. I was just following you."

"You know, Nick, it would be real nice if you had a brain for yourself now and then. Take my advice. Keep your nose clean and steer clear of Thorndike. In about six weeks we'll be at the Sandwich Islands and it's good-bye, *Sea Hawk*. Think you can do that, or is that too tough to figure?" So saying, he pulled his calico curtain closed, shutting me out.

Well. Real brotherly-like.

Little more than a month later, come one afternoon, just as I was climbing down the main shrouds after my spell as lookout, I heard a "Psst!" and saw a white handkerchief fluttering on the end of a fishing pole. The other end of the pole was hidden behind the steerage companionway, beneath the amidship shelter. Though it was a few feet abaft the mainmast and therefore in "officers' country," it seemed as if someone was trying to get my attention. Seeing the mates busy elsewhere, I crept over.

I peered round the companionway. There, crouching, holding the pole, was Elizabeth. "Oh, hello, Nicholas. I was hoping I'd catch a nice tall fish today."

I licked my lips, my heart doing a somersault. "What are you doing?"

"Trying to get your attention, what do you think?"

"What for?"

"I have something for you." She set down the pole, grabbed a sack from behind her, and handed it to me.

"What's in it?"

"Go ahead, open it."

Even before I looked inside, I knew what I'd find. I'd smelled them all afternoon, the aroma wafting up to the mastheads, making my stomach growl and bringing dreams of home. "Gingersnaps," I said, my mouth watering.

"I baked them today with Mother. I made extra for you." She smiled as the breeze ruffled the ribbons on her bonnet. "Thought you might be tired of fo'c'sle food."

I wanted to tell her how much I appreciated her baking extra cookies for me. Actually, what I *really* wanted to tell her was how lovely she looked today. How I liked the way her eyes sparkled when she talked, like sunlight on the ocean. But just as I opened my mouth to thank her, Captain Thorndike emerged from the aft companionway and began peering round as he always did. "I—I've got to go," I blurted, and hurried away, stuffing the bag down my shirt.

When I reached the windlass, I glanced back. Thorndike was staring at me. Elizabeth stood by the steerage companionway where I'd left her, her back to her father, a wounded expression on her face. She waved a tiny wave, only lifting a few fingers.

I turned away, not daring to wave back while the old man's eyes bored holes through me. *Blast Thorndike!* A bitter taste grew in my mouth even as the spicy smell of gingersnaps surrounded me, the cookies warm against my skin.

Only two weeks to go, I thought. *Then Thorndike, Elizabeth, and the* Sea Hawk *will be only a memory.*

CHAPTER 7

*T*he whale's tooth my father had given me was stuffed down my shirt. I also had my ditty box, which held my soap, my comb, my mirror, and whatnot. I couldn't take too much; I didn't want to look suspicious. As it was, I wore my pea jacket to cover it all up, plus two pairs of dungarees, hoping I wouldn't look too stuffy walking round Honolulu.

The *Sea Hawk* was to set sail for the Arctic in the morning. It was the starboard watch's last shore leave. We were to return by nine o'clock that evening, but Dexter and I had other plans.

So after spending more than five months aboard the *Sea Hawk*, enduring much suffering and tribulation, we left the whaler and set off for a spot we'd visited before. Full of grog shops and hotels and seedy characters, the haole district was the perfect place to get lost until the *Sea Hawk* was far away.

It was well after ten o'clock and we were into our third grog shop when a gentleman sitting at a table remarked, "Say, you boys look mighty thirsty."

Dexter and I glanced at each other. It would seem odd to walk into a grog shop and not be thirsty. "Uh—but we don't have much money," said Dexter. "Maybe enough for a drop or two."

The gentleman smiled. "First drink's on me." Dressed in a suit, he was middle-aged, with salt-and-pepper hair. A gold chain draped across his vest front and disappeared into a pocket.

So we spliced the main brace for a spell while I wondered who the gentleman was, why he was in a dirty grog shop, and why he seemed concerned with our thirst. I grew increasingly warm under my several layers of clothes, especially as the man began to ask questions.

"From New Bedford, are you?"

"How did you know?" I asked.

"This place is a regular Tower of Babel. I pride myself on working out the languages and dialects." He lit a pipe. "So, fellows, what ship are you from?"

Dexter frowned, seeming to try and focus. "One of those out there in the harbor, I expect."

The gentleman nodded. "I see, I see. Headed off to the Arctic, then, are you?"

"Sooner or later." Dexter took a swallow of his drink.

"I hear the Arctic can be tough, that lots of boys are deserting to avoid its displeasures. Know anything about that, boys?"

I shook my head, my eyes wide as saucers and innocent as a babe's.

Dexter ran a hand through his sandy hair. "Pardon my asking, Mr.—uh—Mr.—"

"McGuire."

"Mr. McGuire, but who are you, and what concern is it of yours?"

"A fair question, young friend. Allow me to explain." Mr. McGuire withdrew a badge from his pocket. "Constable of the police. I'm on the lookout for deserters. I'm afraid I need to see your passports."

"Passports?" we both asked.

"I'm sure you are aware, no sailors are allowed to spend the night ashore without permission from the governor. If you want to tell me what ship you belong to, I can make certain you're escorted safely aboard. Without a ship, I'll need a passport."

Dexter looked at me, horrified. I knew what he was thinking, for I was thinking the same. We hadn't even run away yet, and already we were caught! Just our luck to sit down to chat with the constable of the police! "Uh—we left our passports outside in my bag. C'mon, Nick, let's go fetch them."

"I—I'm right behind you."

The constable smiled. "Very well, gentlemen, we'll go out together."

When we stood, the constable stood too, and when we hurried to the door, he was behind me, his hand on my shoulder. Outside, a storm had started. Rain fell in torrents. Already streams of mud gushed down the streets. *Now what?* I stepped out into the rain after Dexter. And when the constable hesitated for just a moment, Dexter shoved me, hard. "Run!" he cried. "Run!"

I ran, my heart slamming against my chest.

Behind me I heard a whistle blast. "After them! After them!" From everywhere came the hue and cry of men rushing toward the sound. *Blood and thunder, they're everywhere!*

I raced up one street and down another, Dexter on my heels, the whale's tooth and my ditty box bouncing hard and sharp against me. Rain spattered my face. I could hardly see.

"They went this way!" I heard someone cry.

When I turned to go one way, Dexter yanked me in the opposite direction. "We've got to make it out of the city and into the hills!" Down another street we sprinted, past huts, past homes and stores built of lumber.

By now my lungs burned. *God have mercy!*

Up ahead at one of the houses, a light burned. Beneath the light, people reclined in chairs on a porch. Over the sounds of my ragged breathing, my brogans sucking in and out of the mud, the drone of rain, I heard laughter, voices.

"C'mon," gasped Dexter, "hurry! They're right behind us!"

But as I entered the circle of light, someone grabbed me from behind. I fell, landing hard on the whale's tooth. My breath whooshed out of me. Mud squished in my ear as someone fell on top of me.

Abruptly, the laughter stopped.

My lungs screamed, and I couldn't catch my breath. *I'm caught! I'm caught!* I lay for a while as rain slid round me and seeped into my drawers. *Dexter! What about Dexter? Did he get away?* I hoped so, because I knew what would be waiting for us back at the *Sea Hawk:* Captain Thorndike . . . Punishment . . .

Four men hauled me to my feet, two on each arm. I couldn't see Dexter anywheres.

"Cuff him." The constable was breathing hard, his suit plastered against his body, splattered with mud.

Then came a voice from the porch. "Why, Nicholas Robbins, is that you?"

Elizabeth!

She sat on the porch with her mother, surrounded by several

women. A table was neatly set with teapots and teacups, plates and frosted cake.

"Aye, Miss Thorndike," I said, still gasping for breath, happy to see a friendly face, even if she was the captain's daughter.

The constable bowed. "Sorry to disturb you at your social gathering, ladies, but this young fellow has absconded from his ship. I'm taking him into custody until the proper arrangements can be made."

"Nonsense." Elizabeth stood and smiled sweetly. "Nicholas belongs aboard the *Sea Hawk*. Mother and I sent him into town on an errand so we could have a bit of time to visit our friends, isn't that right, Mother?" Elizabeth smiled briefly at her mother. "Release him, Constable. You've already made quite a mess."

I saw the hesitation on the constable's face. But when Mrs. Thorndike nodded, the constable sighed and said, "Release him, fellows." He tipped his hat. "Ladies. Enjoy the rest of your evening. Sorry to have bothered you. I'll leave this young man in your capable hands."

"Thank you, Constable," said Mrs. Thorndike. "That will be all."

If I had thought I would be bathed, dressed in clean clothes, given a slice of lemon cake, and asked to tell my life story once the constable left, I was sore mistaken.

Mrs. Thorndike immediately demanded that I account for my actions, and when I stumbled over my words, making no sense, meanwhile turning red as Christmas, she declared that she and her daughter must return to the ship immediately.

Elizabeth protested, finally answering with a sullen "Yes, Mother."

I stood in the mud, soaked to the bone, as Mrs. Thorndike said her good-byes to her acquaintances and arranged for transport in a carriage. She had the driver tie me to the carriage with a long rope, then told me to walk beside them and not dally. The rain had stopped as suddenly as it had started. Through the parting clouds, the moon shone bright. Elizabeth cast a sympathetic glance at me before she climbed into the carriage and shut the door. With a cry from the driver and a lurch, we were off. I ran alongside, my wrists tied together.

Twice the carriage got stuck in the mud. I pushed it out as the driver whacked the horse with a whip. The second time, Dexter joined me. Grime coated his face and mud caked his hair.

"Dexter! Why did you come back? Leave now while you can!"

"Shh! I'm here to help you, you fool! Besides, I thought taking you with me was the blasted point of it all."

Even though I wished he hadn't shown up, I was awful glad to see him. After we freed the carriage, he ran next to me, struggling with the knots round my wrist. Mud slimed the rope, wet and slick. Dexter cussed under his breath, spouting words that would make any salty sea dog proud.

Hurry! Hurry!

But it was too late. The carriage rolled to a stop. We'd arrived at the shore, where a boat waited to return us to the ship. Moonlight shone on the water, and dead ahead lay the *Sea Hawk*.

Mrs. Thorndike and Elizabeth alighted from the carriage. "Please convey my gratefulness to Captain Wilson for the use of his carriage," Mrs. Thorndike said to the driver. She then ordered the boatman to untie me, at the same time noticing that there were now two of us. She peered at Dexter. "Why, you're one of the young men aboard my husband's ship, aren't you?"

"Aye. My brother and I, we were just out having a bit of fun. We didn't mean no harm."

She studied us in the moonlight. I'm sure we made some sight, covered with mud and all.

"Mother, please," Elizabeth pleaded. "You know what Father will do."

"Sailors who can't abide by the rules must accept the consequences, Elizabeth. 'Tis a fact of life, or else we have anarchy."

"It won't happen again," I said.

"Of course it won't happen again," she snapped. "We sail in the morning. What were you planning to do, anyways—leave us shorthanded?"

"Why, no, ma'am, we—" began Dexter.

"It shows an utter disregard for the needs of our ship and the needs of our family. Especially as we head off into the Arctic—"

"Mother, please—"

Mrs. Thorndike turned toward her daughter. "And you, Elizabeth. Telling a falsehood in front of my friends and making the constable look like an old fool. I am so ashamed. What will they think of us? And what business is it of yours anyway, young lady? These men work for your father, and they've signed a contract that says so. Now, what kind of captain's wife would I be if I set a bad example by letting them get away with whatever they wanted? And just how did you get to be on a first-name basis with this young man? Oh, never mind! This is all too much. I'm certain your answer would be just another fabrication. Into the boat, all of you, and mind you don't muddy the seats."

No one spoke over the short distance to the ship.

I chewed my fingernails. My palms were clammy. Beads of perspiration glistened on Dexter's forehead. Elizabeth stared at the ship, her face pale as moonlight, while her hands fiddled with the gloves in her lap.

Our boat scraped the side of the *Sea Hawk*. Whale-oil lanterns burned, casting thin white light on the waters.

I heard Captain Thorndike calmly order the bo'sun's chair lowered for the ladies. As for Dexter and me, we waited and then scrambled up the ship's side and onto the deck.

Captain Thorndike was waiting for us, a bullwhip in his hands, a pistol bulging from a holster round his waist. Cole stood beside him.

My mouth went dry. *Blood and thunder. A flogging?*

"Four men from the starboard watch didn't return as ordered," he said.

Dexter and I glanced at each other. *Four men?*

"Deserting be a crime. Punishable by whatever means I deem necessary—"

Elizabeth ran to her father, placing her hands on his shirt-front. "Father, please don't—"

"Elizabeth!" cried her mother. "Go to the cabin at once. You will stay out of the ship's affairs!"

"Mrs. Thorndike!" barked the captain, his scar turning purple. "Control your daughter!"

"Father, please listen. I—"

Thorndike thrust Elizabeth aside. "Strip them for a flogging!" he hollered at Cole.

"Aye, sir!"

"No, Father, please listen to me! I asked them to do an errand—"

While Elizabeth pleaded, Cole grabbed me and stripped off my pea jacket and shirt. My ditty box and whale's tooth fell to the deck with a clatter.

There was a sudden silence.

Captain Thorndike walked over and picked up my ditty box. "Tell me, Elizabeth, what sailor goes on an errand for ye while carrying his ditty box? What was he a-going to do for ye, give ye a shave? Go below this instant. I'll have words with ye later."

I heard Elizabeth scream, "No! No!" as they strung me by my wrists from the rigging.

The captain swung back and lashed the whip. *No!* Pain seared me, white-hot, burning. Again, again. A strange sound was coming from somewhere, and I realized it came from my own throat.

A week after my flogging, as the *Sea Hawk* sliced through the water toward the Arctic, tossing a fine mist over her decks, Duff, the steward, pressed a folded piece of paper into my hand.

It was a letter from Elizabeth. Her writing swirled across the page without a splotch of ink anywhere.

> *Dear Nicholas,*
>
> *Finally they have stopped watching me so closely and I am able to get a letter to you. Duff says you and Dexter are some better. I'm glad. My parents are still furious with me, of course. Mother lectures me night and day and has given me extra lessons in the consequences of lying. Father says I'm a willful, disobedient child, and in need of firm discipline. I don't*

mean to be willful and disobedient, but sometimes I get so angry. Prince Albert is my only true companion. He loves it when I play the piano. Have you heard me play "Do You Ever Think of Me?" Whenever you hear it, I am thinking of you. Please write me back.

Affectionately,
Elizabeth

I had, in fact, heard this song tinkling from the stern many a time. During the dogwatch, as the men lazed about the windlass, smoking and yarning and sharpening harpoons, I'd hear the piano. The men would grow quiet, listening. Sometimes I'd hear a young voice singing as well, wafting like a breeze through the evening air, sweet and tremulous, and I knew it was Elizabeth.

"Then tell me—do you ever,
When my bark is on the sea,
Give a thought to her who never
Can cease to think of thee?"

After sniffing the letter (it smelled of lilacs), I stowed it in my sea chest, planning to burn it in the next trypot fire. I didn't dare write her in return. Jerusalem crickets, she was Thorndike's *daughter*! What if the old man found letters to Elizabeth with my name signed below? He'd boil my oil in the trypots.

Duff passed Elizabeth's letters to me every day after that, each one imploring me to write back. I felt horribly guilty for not doing so and wished she'd stop writing me. I almost dreaded seeing Duff approach. Once I even ran and hid, but he found me. There are only so many places a sailor can hide on a ship while on duty.

Then the letters stopped. One day they were coming as regular as ships' bells; the next day, nothing. I was surprised at my disappointment when Duff only poured me coffee. What, no letter? By the time a cold rainy day in early June rolled round, it had been a week since I'd received a letter, heard her play the piano, or sing. A week! Why had she stopped writing? Didn't she like me anymore? Was she writing to someone else instead? I realized I'd been counting on her letters. They were funny and chatty, and gave me something to do. That afternoon, I reread all her letters and decided maybe I wouldn't burn them after all. Besides, they smelled of lilacs.

We lay to off the coast of Siberia, beset by fogs and snow squalls while the previous winter's ice circled and bumped against the *Sea Hawk*'s copper sheathing. Sometimes we heard spouts but couldn't see them, and didn't dare to lower on account of the fog. Other times, when the fog lifted, we saw the sails of some sixty whalers or more. Then, if a whale came along, it was a mad dash to be the first upon it. We had yet to fetch ourselves a whale, though we'd been here three blasted weeks already. And without whale oil bursting our hold, we couldn't go home.

I avoided Thorndike. Not only did I hate him, but one look at me and, certain, he'd know his daughter was writing me letters. *Maybe the old man caught her,* I thought as I rowed across the sea, chasing a polar whale. *Maybe he took away her ink and paper and that's why she hasn't written. Maybe he's just biding his time before he tosses me overboard or 'poons me with an iron.*

"Mind yourself," grumbled Briggs from his position as midship oarsman.

I realized my rhythm was off. "Sorry." Rain streamed off my sou'wester and puddled on my lap. Three polar whales meandered slowly to the northeast, and we followed their telltale V-shaped spouts.

Polar whales were fat things, wrapped in a blanket of blubber so they could stay warm in seas colder than ice. They didn't have teeth, at least not normal teeth. They swam with their mouths open wide enough to admit a horse and carriage, scooping up giant mouthfuls of water. Then they strained the water out through long, hairy, bonelike slats. They swallowed what was left—tiny creatures, each no bigger than a bug. But there were thousands of creatures. Millions. Making for one monstrous gulp.

"Ice off the port bow," whispered Sweet. "Pull two, boys, pull two. All of ye now, pull with a will. Can't let these other measly excuses for men beat us now, can we? We've got a reputation to uphold, and a nasty one at that. Think of one of them fat oily beasts a-lying in our hold. Think of home, boys. We'll be that much closer."

I gritted my teeth and pulled hard. My stomach growled. My back ached. Despite my sou'wester and oilskins, I felt damp through. *And what I wouldn't give for a slice of Aunt Agatha's quince pie smothered with hot cream! I wonder what Aunt Agatha's having for supper tonight. Baked beans and codfish chowder? Maybe hot coddled apples. What's Elizabeth eating, I wonder? Iced lemon cake? Pie? Hot biscuits smothered with butter and jam? Roasted chicken falling off the bone? Certain she doesn't eat salt beef and hard bread day after day, with coffee hot enough to scald the devil.*

So busy was I with my daydreaming, I didn't notice that the rain had stopped or that the fog had rolled in until it was thick as chowder. I could barely see Dexter sitting one seat in front of me, or Sweet facing us in the stern, scowling through the mist, muttering, "Blasted pea soup." Mist crawled over my face and under my collar, cold as a wet fish. I shivered. Sometimes the fog could stay for days and days.

We stopped rowing and listened for the sound of our ship, calling us back. Three blasts with the foghorn, followed by two rings of the bell and one shot from the pistol. But the fog was filled with blasts, shots, and rings from dozens of ships, making it impossible to tell which signals were the *Sea Hawk*'s.

"Looks like we're stuck here," said Briggs.

"Not to worry, though, boys," said Sweet. "We've got all we need to survive for weeks. Captain made sure of that."

"Weeks!" I croaked.

"Just an expression, just an expression, Bones, don't be getting yourself in a flurry of feathers. Soon as the fog lifts, why, we'll spy the *Sea Hawk* right away, mark my words." With that, Sweet opened the lantern-keg and broke out the hard bread—a square sailor's biscuit baked so hard it could put out an eye.

Though it wasn't a hot buttered biscuit with jam, I wolfed it down, wishing for more.

Dexter moved to sit next to me. After all, we weren't rowing or doing much of anything, so it was all right to move round some. He rubbed his hands together, blew in them, and then pulled on his gloves. He wiped his nose on his sleeve. "I figure it'll take thirty polar whales and then we can go home."

Garret answered from his position in the bow. Ever since he'd begun bunking in steerage and doing the duties of a harpooneer, the only time we really had together was when we chased whales. "Some ships fetch twenty in a year's time," he was saying; "others take a whale a year. Luck of the draw, I reckon. Two ships can hunt side by side. One comes away with her hold busting at the seams; the other ship's empty as a whiskey barrel at an Irish jig."

"Making excuses, Carrot Sticks?" said Briggs.

"Don't sound to me like excuses," Irish said, "sounds like rotten luck. The *Sea Hawk*'s mighty unlucky, if it's me you're asking. Been gone near three-quarters of a year, we have, and we've only three whales to account for. If what ye say is true, lads, it'll be almost five years before we can even start for home."

I drooped over my oar. "I'd be almost twenty-one years old."

"If ye live that long," said Briggs under his breath.

I ignored him. Briggs was always trying to provoke me. I wanted to tell him to mind his own ugly business, but we didn't need a fistfight in the whaleboat. We'd end up in the water and get frozen solid.

"Captain Thorndike don't care how long we're out here," Briggs continued, his voice a mite whiny, muffled in the fog. "He's got his family along. He's got good food. Not this hard bread and salt beef that would choke a dog. Then, like he's the king of his kingdom, he throws us some rice and bugs once a week like that's good enough for the likes of us."

"Now, Briggs," said Sweet, "don't be a-riling folks. Just simmer down, or I'll have to dunk ye overboard to cool off."

"Besides, Briggs," said Dexter. "Seems like the food was just fine to you until you got demoted."

"Why, you little—"

"Enough!" hollered Sweet.

The boat settled into silence. Pistol shots and bells and horns still sounded all round us. Irish crossed his arms and settled down as if for a nap. Through the fog I vaguely saw Garret sprawled against the bow, chewing on a toothpick. "I'm just saying," said Briggs after a while, "I'm hungry all the time. The captain don't feed us near enough."

"Why don't you go talk to him about it?" asked Dexter.

"What, and get my face smashed again?" Briggs' voice was laced with anger. "I'm tired of it all. The old man has everything he wants, while we do all his dirty work."

"Captain's got his own troubles," said Sweet as he lit his pipe. The tobacco glowed orange through the fog.

"Pardon me if I don't feel sorry for him," said Briggs.

"Fact is," continued Sweet, "his wife's taken ill. His daughter, too."

I sat up, my breath catching. "What do you mean?"

"Just heard they had some fever. Cole says they're at death's door." Sweet coughed out a lungful of smoke. "I always figured women was too weak for the whaling life. Injures their delicate constitutions."

I lay back, the blood draining from my face.

"Oh, by the way, Bones," said Sweet, reaching into his coat and pulling out a folded paper. "Duff said to give this to ye. He's been a little under the weather himself. Sorry, but I've had it a few days."

It was a letter, sealed with red wax, stamped with a curlicued *E*.

I took it from Sweet, turned away from Dexter, and opened it. The handwriting was scrawling, shaky, ink splotches here and there.

> *Dear Nicholas,*
> *Please come see me.*
> *Affectionately, Elizabeth*

Hands trembling, I looked up, aware that everyone was staring at me, expecting me to say something.

I stowed the letter in my coat pocket and looked away. Blood pounded in my ears.

Dexter whispered, "Don't even think it."

I ignored him, staring out into the fog, thinking, *Soon as I get aboard the* Sea Hawk, *I'll go see Elizabeth. Thorndike can go to hell.*

The next day, when the fog lifted, we returned to the *Sea Hawk*.

A whale was alongside, caught by one of the other three whaleboats. As I stepped aboard, commands fell fast and furious. Men ran here, then there. Heavy chains clanked and rattled across a deck coated with oil and blood.

Thorndike stood by the gangway talking with Cole.

It was a perfect opportunity to slip below.

With a quick glance round, down the companionway I crept. At the bottom was a small door. Hands sweaty, I unlatched the door and peered into the captain's cabin, half expecting Mrs. Thorndike to be standing there ready to scream. But the cabin was empty. I stepped inside and shut the door.

The cabin was a far cry from the fo'c'sle: whitewashed, low-ceilinged, with a red velvet settee, a captain's desk, a stove, and a piano. Doors led off from the cabin. I figured Elizabeth would be in one of the two port cabins.

But which one?

Taking a deep breath, I opened the forward door an inch and put my eye to the crack. The cabin was small, no bigger than my closet in New Bedford. Whitewashed like the main cabin, it contained a dresser, a closet, a washstand, and a single bed. Elizabeth lay sleeping, her cat curled at the foot of the bed. Strewn across her pillow and plastered in wet strands against her face, her hair looked caught in a tempest. I heard the pant of her breath.

As quiet as I could, I opened the door wider to step inside. Suddenly, my heart dropped to my brogans, for I heard the tromp of heavy footsteps on the companionway. *Blood and thunder! Someone's coming!*

aster than I've ever moved before, I dashed into Elizabeth's room, opened her closet, and squeezed inside, banging my knee and bumping my head. I pulled the closet door shut just as I heard someone enter the captain's cabin. There was the sound of papers rustling. A grunt. Heavy footsteps again. Then I heard the creak of a door being opened.

"Catharine?" At the sound of the voice, my blood froze. It was Captain Thorndike! "Catharine, dear? I've come to check on ye. Be ye sleeping?" His voice surprised me, for it was as tender as if his wife were a babe. I heard the sound of a bed squeaking and knew he must have sat next to his wife.

"Catharine? My love, answer me. Answer me, love." A pause. A rustle of bedclothes.

Again the bed squeaked. For a long time, silence. The pounding of my heart. Then an anguished cry. Like a rock scraped across a pane of glass.

Another cry. And there began an awful wailing. "No! No! God, no! Please don't take her! Not Catharine!" cried Thorndike, his voice cracked and dreadful to hear. "My love, my life. I need you! I need you!" He burst into deep, wretched sobs I'd never heard a man cry before.

Tears sprang to my eyes. Mrs. Thorndike was dead, no doubt. Elizabeth's mother. I could imagine the sorrow, for I hadn't forgotten the day I learned my father had died. It was a deep, jagged pain that lay buried a hundred layers down but was there nonetheless. Much as I hated Captain Thorndike, hated him for all his cruelty, for the scars on my back, I was sorry for him too. It was confusing, so I just stood and cried and cried, wiping my nose on my sleeve, not caring that Dexter would roll his eyes and call me a sissy girl and a blasted idiot besides.

Then Elizabeth spoke. "Father? . . . Father?"

There came a creak of someone rising from the bed. Heavy footsteps.

"Is she dead?" Elizabeth asked in a whisper.

There was no sound. I imagined Captain Thorndike standing in the doorway, his face contorted with weeping, staring at his daughter with eyes turned red. I started to cry again, silently, trying not to sniff. "Aye," he finally answered, "she's dead. And you've yourself to thank for it, upsetting her the way ye did. You've sent her to an early grave."

I heard a gasp, a cry, and then sounds of Elizabeth's weeping. Of Captain Thorndike in the main cabin. A door opening. Closing. The thud of footsteps and the creak of stairs. And Elizabeth weeping. And weeping.

I fumbled in the dark for the closet latch.

"Who's there?" came Elizabeth's frightened voice.

I fumbled a bit more. *If I can just get out of the blasted closet . . .*

"Who's there?"

I pushed hard against the door and found the latch at the same time. Out I tumbled in a cascade of clothing and books and shoes. I whapped my chin on the washstand on the way down and skinned my elbows as I landed.

"Nicholas!"

It wasn't exactly the entrance I'd imagined as I'd lain awake all night in the whaleboat. I removed a petticoat from atop my face. "Sorry," I mumbled, sitting up.

But she didn't laugh at me. Instead, tears slipped down her cheeks and her lips trembled. "Did you hear? Mother's dead. She's dead. And Father hates me." With that, she laid her face in her hands and sobbed.

I got up and closed the cabin door. Hesitating, I sat beside her. She leaned against me. I felt the burn of her fever. The moisture. The thin gauze of her nightgown. I hesitated again but then wrapped my arms round her. She cried and cried while I stroked her hair, saying, "Don't cry, Elizabeth. Don't cry." And as her head settled against my chest, I knew. The realization struck me like a harpoon driven deep into my heart: I was in love with the captain's daughter.

We lay at anchor among the ice floes, silent, our flag at half-mast while they buried Mrs. Thorndike on the Siberian coast. For a whole hour, we just watched from the rail. Then, after Thorndike and the mates returned to the *Sea Hawk*, ships' captains stopped by to pay their respects, bringing wives and children. It was a solemn affair. Black suits, black dresses, black gloves and veils. People sitting prim and proper, ferried in boats that passed between ships.

"We're so sorry to hear of your wife's passing. She was a dear soul."

"I hear your daughter's sick as well. Give her our wishes for a speedy recovery."

"She'll be missed, certain. 'Twarn't no one like Catharine Thorndike. She could bake the best green-currant pie in Massachusetts. Shame she didn't give me her recipe."

"Rest assured, Ebenezer, she's in a better place."

I could practically hear the old man's teeth grind, sensing his impatience to be rid of everyone even as he offered his visitors more hot tea.

Sure enough, after four days of visits, he ordered us to up anchor and head north, saying he was sick of sharing every whale chase with every ship ever built, sick of them all. We sailed in the company of the *Merimont,* whose captain was said to be Thorndike's good friend from way back when.

I hadn't told Dexter what I'd done. Where I'd been and what I'd heard. But he looked at me as if he knew anyways. Caution blazed in his eyes as if he were a lighthouse warning an unwary ship away from the rocks. I always turned away, pretending I didn't notice. *Just because you're older doesn't mean you know everything. Besides, you wouldn't understand.*

Hoping for a glimpse of Elizabeth, I traded crow's nest duty for helmsman's duty whenever someone was willing, throwing in a plug of tobacco or a plum duff every now and then to sweeten the deal. For two hours at a stretch, I followed Thorndike's orders. Most times he stood at the foremast crow's nest, spyglass to his eye, hollering from aloft through a middleman: "Steady!" "Starboard!" "Luff! Luff!" "Steady now!" as we steered between the ice floes. Dangerous work it was. By the end of a two-hour shift, my stomach was in knots and I was sore disappointed that I hadn't seen Elizabeth. Was she better? Was she dying?

Meanwhile, we sailed with the *Merimont* between St. Lawrence Island and the mainland. We anchored for a time in St. Lawrence Bay along the Siberian coast. As a thick fog settled round us, natives came aboard to trade. They were short, chunky people, smiling, with brown eyes and straight black hair, smelling of grease. They offered furs and ivory in trade for tobacco. All the natives chewed and smoked tobacco—even the children. I imagined Aunt Agatha having an absolute conniption if she saw such goings-on. (I'd secretly tried chewing tobacco once, but after choking and turning green as seaweed decided it was better to get rid of it altogether.) I traded one plug of tobacco for a reindeer fur and another for a walrus tusk.

That evening in the fo'c'sle, as I began to carve my tusk, Briggs was going on and on about how the natives were filthy beasts, how you could smell them before you could see them. How they were stupid and no-account and hardly better than animals. How if it weren't for us Yankees, they would have remained savages forever. We were doing them a favor, he said. Dexter told Briggs to shut up, that he was sick of hearing Briggs' whiny voice, that there was no one on earth smellier and stupider than Briggs himself. Of course, they went at it hammer and tongs. But I couldn't help wondering if maybe Briggs was right, for I discovered the natives had sold me a broken walrus tusk, cleverly repaired with rivets and smoothed over with seal fat.

I'd been cheated.

While the ship was stuck in the fog, the mates kept us busy. We spliced worn-out rigging, scraped rust from anchors and chains, made fresh sets of ratlines, and scrubbed the latrines. Every day, regardless of how cold it was, barefooted, pants rolled up, armed with scrub brooms, we swabbed the decks as the mates sloshed bucketfuls of icy seawater in front of us, telling us to look lively or the captain would warm our hides the hard way.

Often, melting our middles like butter on a hot griddle, we'd hear Garret singing as he sharpened his lances and irons, oiling them till they glistened. Garret had a warm, rich voice, perfect for ballads, and it made our work seem bearable, made it seem as if one day we'd all be home, with money in our pockets, never cold again.

One day, our watch was tarring the standing rigging when Irish jabbed my ribs. He winked, put a finger to his mouth for silence, and pointed. There, snoozing like a babe atop the fore hatch, was Briggs, his bucket of tar beside him. I nudged Dexter, who stopped midwhistle, a right devilish grin spreading across his face. Then, with a wink at me and Irish, Dexter crept over and gingerly smeared tar on Briggs' nose and cheeks. Briggs mumbled, snorted, and rolled over, getting right comfy once again. The three of us quickly got to tarring, trying hard not to split our sides while looking industrious and innocent.

Suddenly, Briggs' eyes popped open. Like a corpse rising from the grave, he sat up straight, touching the tar on his cheeks, his nose. His eyes narrowed when he spied us tarring the rigging so innocent-like. He jumped to his feet. "Why, you—"

"Ah, shut yer fat gob," muttered Irish.

"You—you tarred me!"

"Tell it to someone who cares," said Dexter. "The captain, maybe."

"Gee whittaker," I couldn't help blurting, "you look real nice, Briggs."

Just then, Thorndike stepped out from behind the tryworks, his pipe clamped between his teeth.

"What's going on here?" demanded Thorndike.

Briggs pointed at us. "They tarred me!"

"And how do ye suppose they did that?"

Briggs blinked, and his lip twitched. "Uh—I—uh—"

"Ye were sleeping on watch, weren't ye?"

"Uh—I—no—"

"What, ye just let them tar your face?"

"No, sir, I—" Briggs' words evaporated like water in the hot sun. His eyes widened as Thorndike took hold of the tar brush and began smearing tar all over Briggs. And not just his cheeks and nose, but his ears, his hair, his face, his mouth . . .

"Sir, sir, please stop."

"Shut your mouth, sailor."

"I can't breathe. It's hot, it's hot!"

"I said shut your mouth."

Meanwhile, Irish, Dexter, and I were tarring like crazy, as if we'd never dream of sleeping on watch, or globbing someone's face with tar. My knees shook, and the Arctic air suddenly seemed hot.

After tarring every bit of Briggs' skin, Thorndike kicked him on his backside. Briggs tumbled to his knees.

"Bread and water for the next week, sailor, for sleeping on watch. Now go clean yourself up, you sorry waste of skin."

To my relief, Thorndike turned and left, the thunk of his heavy boots moving aft. The three of us glanced at one another. This wasn't exactly what we'd planned. Irish hesitated and then went to help Briggs.

"Leave me alone!" Briggs screamed when Irish touched him. He stumbled to his feet and, after blindly searching for the fo'c'sle companionway, disappeared below.

It took Briggs two days to clean himself of tar. He shaved his hair completely, and his skin turned a bright crusty red that blended nice with his pimples. To my surprise, though, he never said anything about it; didn't throw cockroaches at me anymore, elbow my temple in the rigging, or go at it hammer and tongs with Dexter. He just did his work, tight-lipped and alone, and he didn't lie down for any more snoozes, either. We all agreed we liked him better this way.

"Tarred the snot out of him," said Dexter.

In late June when the fog lifted, we raised anchor and beat our way north through the Bering Strait under double-reefed top-sails. The wind howled as it ripped through the narrow strip of water, funneled between two masses of land. Screeching birds circled the rocky cliffs of the nearby islands. Whenever I lay in my bunk now, cold air swirling round the fo'c'sle, I curled under my reindeer fur and dreamed of home, mourning the loss of the carved tooth my father had given me (I'd lost it on the day of my flogging) and wondering if Elizabeth was still alive, my chest aching with the desire to see her again.

Then, one day, when a gale came screaming out of the north, we lost Irish overboard. One moment he was beside me, standing on the footrope of the main topgallant yard, and the next he wasn't.

Gone.

Those below saw him fall, cartwheeling through the air. They hove to and lowered a boat into the crashing waves, but it was too late. I saw him thrashing in the water, but when they cast him a life buoy, he couldn't grasp it. Hands too frozen, they told me later. Body paralyzed with cold. While I watched from the yard, horrified, Irish sank beneath the sea.

Gone.

We held a little ceremony. We were surprised to learn that Irish's real name was Sean Donovan. We said a prayer and sang some hymns. Afterward, the order was given to "brace up and haul aft!" and soon the *Sea Hawk* sailed by the wind again. It was back to business. As if Sean Donovan had never lived. As if Sean Donovan had never walked the decks, slid out on a footrope, or taken a trick at the wheel.

Death was that way, at sea.

I snugged my woolen cap over my head and yanked my collar up round my neck. I squinted in the bright sun, the wind stealing my breath away in cloudy snatches.

It was now my trick at the wheel, so I walked behind Dexter and took hold of the spokes the way I'd been taught.

"Full and by," said Dexter as he moved away.

"Full and by," I repeated, aware that the second mate listened to be sure I had repeated the ship's heading correctly. We sailed north of the Bering Strait, occasionally chasing a polar whale, still with no luck, although the *Merimont* had caught three. We cruised first one way, then another, with no particular direction in mind, on the lookout twenty-four hours a day, since the sun didn't set in these parts in July.

"Full and by!" barked the second mate in my ear.

I jumped and spun the wheel to starboard. "Full and by, sir!" I cried. I brought her to, and the sails tightened.

"Steady as she goes," said the second mate.

"Steady as she goes, sir!"

Ten minutes later, Captain Thorndike came up on deck, leading Elizabeth by the arm. I near swallowed my tonsils. *Elizabeth!*

She looked pale, thin as a heron's leg. Dressed thick in a coat of reindeer fur and boots of sealskin, no doubt purchased from the natives. She peeped at me from behind a hood fringed with wolverine, giving me a smile so slight I didn't think anyone else would know it was meant to be a smile, but *I* knew. Prince Albert twined about her ankles, mewing.

She sat upon the deck chair offered by the second mate, told her father she was just fine, thank you very much, and submitted to having a blanket tucked round her neck, after which the old man disappeared below again. Prince Albert jumped onto Elizabeth's lap just as Cook brought her a mug of hot chocolate. She removed her deerskin mittens and wrapped her slender fingers round the mug as wisps of steam curled into the crisp air. My mouth watered at the warm, rich smell of chocolate.

Second Mate Walker straightened from holding Elizabeth's chair and glanced at me. He strode over with a purpose and said quietly in a hard tone, "Keep your eyes straight ahead, sailor. Remember your duties and your course."

I tore my gaze away from Elizabeth, realizing I'd let the ship fall off. *Don't that beat all!* I thought as I brought the ship to. *Elizabeth is recovered!* A warm feeling grew from my toes to my nose and I wanted to leap for joy.

Just then, a cry came from the foremast crow's nest. "Ice ahead, sir!"

"Where away?" shouted the second mate.

"Everywhere, sir! And covered with strange beasts, sir!"

Captain Thorndike bounded up the companionway ladder, his face emotionless beneath his gray-streaked beard. After gazing through his glass, he said, "Walruses." He strode to the foremast to guide us through the ice.

They smelled like pigs, the walruses. Their stink curled my nose worse than Dexter's dirty underdrawers. Piled atop the melting ice floes lay hundreds, maybe thousands of the beasts, bellowing, trumpeting, snorting. As the *Sea Hawk* drew near, they lifted their massive heads to peer at us with tiny bloodshot eyes. The bulls were massive, their tusks up to a yard in length, their whiskers like bristle brushes. Fat, round calves nursed from the cows, pulling away to stare at us, their mouths milky white.

"They're amazing," breathed Elizabeth.

I hadn't realized she was beside me, but aye, she now stood at my elbow. Everyone on the ship seemed mesmerized by the walruses, so no one noticed the captain's daughter standing next to me. Except me, that is. Even over the stench of walruses, I smelled a hint of lilacs.

"Maybe we'll fetch a whale today," Elizabeth said softly. "It would be nice to fill our hold and go home. I swear I hate this place. It's wretched and lonely with Mother gone. I miss her."

Just as I was about to tell her how sorry I was about her mother, Prince Albert leapt atop the rail. I'd seen him do it many a time before and hadn't given it a thought. Today, though, he suddenly became a blur of claws and legs, scrabbling for balance.

Then, with a howl, eyes huge, he slid over the edge and disappeared.

"Albert!" shrieked Elizabeth. She rushed to the rail. "Albert!"

I heard splashing. Howls. The walruses erupted in a chorus of bellowing, diving off the ice floes.

"Nick!" Elizabeth screamed, her face stricken. "Lower a boat!"

"Belay that order!" barked Captain Thorndike, striding aft. "You'll stay at the helm and keep the ship on course as ordered, sailor!"

I nodded, speechless.

"But Father, he's drowning!"

"Walker! Take over at the foremast."

"Aye, aye, sir!"

"Steady as she goes," said Thorndike calmly. He faced forward, clasped his hands behind his back, and looked straight ahead.

Out of the corner of my eye, I saw Elizabeth staring at her father, her eyes round with disbelief. Then, before I knew what was happening, Elizabeth shrugged out of her fur coat, climbed over the rail, and jumped overboard, her white dress and blond hair billowing upward as she disappeared.

CHAPTER
II

"Elizabeth!" I screamed, leaving the wheel and starting for the rail.

Behind me, I heard shouts. "Man overboard! Man overboard!" "Hard down!" "Let go the life buoy!"

Suddenly, Thorndike was in front of me. "Back to your station, helmsman! Hard down the wheel! That's an order!" I tried to move round him, to reach the rail, to save Elizabeth, but before I could even blink he smashed me upside my jaw, his fist hard as a brick. I spun with the impact and collapsed to the deck.

My vision swam. I tasted blood. *Elizabeth!* Before I could get my feet under me, Thorndike hauled me to my feet and set me before the wheel. "Hard down!"

Then he was gone, and Garret was there helping me turn the wheel.

"Let flow the head sheets!" Cole ordered. "Haul in spanker boom. . . ."

I shook my head to clear the dizziness, stunned with the pain in my jaw. I heard the rattle of blocks and the splash of a boat hitting the water. Mainsail aback, the *Sea Hawk* finally drifted to a stop.

"You okay?" whispered Garret.

I nodded, still unable to speak.

"They're fetching Elizabeth, don't you worry none."

Then, from the sea, I heard crying. Coughing. "He's gone. Albert's gone. You let him die. I hate you! You're a horrid father!"

A silence settled, thick as fog. Beside me, Garret shifted his feet, cleared his throat. After a moment, a bo'sun's chair was lowered, and Elizabeth was brought aboard. Hair in strings, lips blue, teeth chattering, dripping wet, she disentangled herself from the bo'sun's chair and, without a word to anyone, went below. One by one, several men, including Dexter and Thorndike, clambered over the ship's side and onto the deck.

Thorndike was breathing hard, his scar a vivid purple, his face like a gathering storm. "Cook, make Miss Elizabeth some tea, or some hot chocolate. Blood and thunder, I don't care what you make her."

"Aye, sir."

"Duff, stoke the stove in the cabin and bring her some dry towels."

"Aye, sir."

"Cole, man the mastheads."

"Aye, sir."

Then, still breathing hard, he strode toward me while removing the pistol from his holster. Light flashed as he swung the pistol, bashing the side of my skull. I crumpled to the deck, my bones turned to noodles. I saw stars and legs all round me.

"What use is a helmsman," Thorndike was screaming, "if he can't follow orders?"

I felt a sharp kick in my ribs.

Not again. I groaned. *I hate this ship. I despise Thorndike. He's a monster. . . .*

Another kick. Another. Then I heard the sound of a hammer being cocked on a pistol.

"Uh, Captain—" Dexter said.

I heard the captain breathing hard, the puff and bellow of walruses, the bleat of little Ninny. I saw brogans scraping the deck. Feet shifting. Felt everyone staring at me while hot blood pooled in my ear.

Then came the cry, *"There she blo-o-o-ows!"*

"Where away?"

"Broad off the lee beam, sir! Several of them, sir!"

The captain released a long breath. "Into the boats, boys, and after them. We've got whales to catch."

"Remember a while back when we spent two days ashore in our whaleboat?" Dexter whispered. "When we couldn't find our way back to the ship until the fog lifted?"

It was the day after my pistol-whipping. I lay in my bunk, my hatred of Thorndike like rat poison in my mouth. I'd been crazy to ever feel sorry for that man. My head roared. The upper bunk spun. I closed my eyes and gritted my teeth to stop its spinning. "Aye."

"Next time that happens, we'll wait for everyone to fall asleep, and then we'll take off. They won't take the time to find us. We'll cover our tracks."

I groaned. "I think I'm going to throw up."

Dexter thrust a bucket into my hands. Nothing but dry heaves. A glob of spit. Afterward, I lay back on my bunk. "What about Elizabeth?"

"Face it, Nick, you'll never see her again. At least not on this voyage. Word has it the old man's locked her in her cabin and she won't see the light of day until we're home in New Bedford."

"But she—"

Dexter patted my shoulder. "She's safe, Nick. Safer than you, by thunder. Someday when you're back in New Bedford, you can see her again. But you can't see her if you're dead. Besides, all the fellows are saying you're a blasted fool for meddling with Thorndike's daughter. Once he finds out, your life won't be worth a bucket of pig squat."

Waiting for an opportunity to escape was like waiting for our hair to grow.

We chased whales, aye, but either we were too far from land or the weather was too clear for us to take refuge in anything other than the whaler. Meanwhile, the *Sea Hawk* sailed northeast along Alaska's northwest coast, caught in a swift current.

Dexter and I held back portions of our food now at each meal. I was always hungry, my stomach as empty as Briggs' head. We stored the food in Dexter's sea chest, away from rats, cockroaches, and hungry shipmates.

In between chasing whales, in between goat duty, I was set to work with Dexter scraping gum from the slabs of baleen—the hairy, bonelike slats that grew like teeth in the mouths of polar whales. Each piece was flat and long, some of them twice as long as I was tall. Baleen was as valuable as whale oil; it was used in ladies' corsets, buggy whips, hats, shoehorns, brushes, and umbrellas, to name a few. It was tough, like fingernails or horses' hooves.

As Dexter and I scraped gum hour after boring hour, we whispered about our escape, planning every last detail, gazing at the land whenever we caught glimpse of it. Empty, treeless, flat, it stretched forever. Despite our fancy plans, the thought of running away across that vast expanse left my stomach in my toes.

Whenever I had a moment to myself, I spent my time carving. Carving figures out of ivory or wood gave me something to do besides think of escape. And as figures formed in my hands, I felt almost normal. Life was good, none of the rest of this was real, nothing bad could possibly happen. I carved an ivory figure of Prince Albert and gave it to Duff to give to Elizabeth to remember him by. She wrote a letter saying thank you, that she'd treasure it always and that she cried for Prince Albert every day. Letter clutched to my chest, I fell asleep in my bunk, dreaming of drowning cats, lilacs, and Briggs' ugly mug looming over me.

As August slipped into September, Dexter and I became right anxious. Thorndike and the captain of the *Merimont* pushed their ships ever north, farther north than anyone had gone before, according to Garret. It was uncharted territory, and winter could come at any time in these parts. Dexter and I weren't the only ones glancing at shore, wondering if we'd ever see home again.

Finally, in mid-September, to everyone's relief, Thorndike ordered the *Sea Hawk* south. It was slow going, for now we fought the current, which was swifter than we'd first believed. Even so, Dexter and I knew there would soon come a day when the *Sea Hawk* would sail through the strait and head back to the Sandwich Islands. What, then? We both knew the answer, for Garret had already told us: we'd spend another winter season hunting sperm whales in the Pacific and then go back to the Arctic for another summer season.

I chewed my fingernails down to the nubs. I would have chewed my toenails too, but the rats had taken care of my toenails handily.

Then, finally, there came a day in late September when our fortunes changed.

It was a beauty of a whale—fifty-five feet long, weighing fifty tons, likely to yield at least a hundred barrels of oil plus a thousand pounds of baleen. Worth a fortune. But while my shipmates congratulated each other, I glanced longingly toward shore. Wind slapped my aching ears. The coast was some distance away, but I could see it—low, flat, white with snow. . . . *Freedom. Freedom from Thorndike.*

Again we'd failed.

Dexter kicked the mainmast and hopped around a bit on one foot, cursing the world, his toe, the *Sea Hawk,* and all whales in general. "That was our last chance," he said, cursing again, kicking the chicken coop this time as chickens squawked and feathers danced in the wind. "We're stuck. Do you hear me, Nick? We're stuck for another year."

"Aye, I hear you," I said as the *Merimont* luffed alongside.

"Our hold is full!" the captain of the *Merimont* hollered through his speaking trumpet. "We've enough oil and are heading home!" Sailors lined the *Merimont*'s rails, grinning. A few tossed their caps into the air and cheered.

The Merimont*'s hold is full. They're going home. They're leaving us.*

"We'll be right behind ye," Thorndike replied through his speaking trumpet. "We've got to finish cutting in and trying out our whale."

"Aye! But be quick about it." The captain of the *Merimont* glanced over his shoulder. A thin line of white stretched across the northern horizon. I'd noticed it a while back but didn't know what it was. "The pack ice is a-coming. If it gets here before ye get out, my friend, you'll be stuck. I fear winter has us by the throat at last!" As if to prove his point, his cap flew off his head and into the water with a fierce blast of wind. Then, after the captains promised to look each other up in New Bedford and traded other such pleasantries, the *Merimont* was off.

"I have a bad feeling about this," murmured Dexter as we watched the *Merimont*'s sails fill for home.

"Nonsense," said Sweet, overhearing. "We'll be in his wake before ye know what hit ye. Now heave and pawl, men! Look lively!"

Within an hour the sky blackened and the wind increased until it howled like a pack of wolves. Ice and oil coated the decks. We slipped and slid as waves, white-capped and furious, tossed the ship round and washed over the men cutting in the whale. They clung to the cutting stage for dear life, sometimes buried up to their necks in foam. In the trough of the waves, they hacked the blubber, their lips blue. The trypots threw up huge clouds of steam and oil droplets as seawater swirled round the fires.

Finally, letting fly a string of bloodcurdling curses, the old man ordered the whale cut loose, the tryworks closed down, and all men aboard even though we weren't half finished.

We'd been anchored a couple miles from land in less than fifteen fathoms of water, and now we drew up anchor, double-reefed our topsails, hauled taut the braces, and dashed madly after the *Merimont*. A leaden, heavy sky pressed down. Snow whipped round us, gusting over our decks. Ninny bleated. Chickens squawked. Spray flew the length of the *Sea Hawk* as she plunged through the waves, groaning, burying her rails in water.

Although we could no longer see it, to our port was the shore. To our starboard was the polar ice pack, bearing down on us like a horde of bloodthirsty pirates. We sailed blind, knowing that if the ice reached us before we could claw our way out of here, we'd be crushed between land and ice. Like being smashed between a hammer and anvil.

I was checking the lashings on the port-bow boat, as ordered, when someone tapped my shoulder. It was Cole. Water sluiced off his sou'wester. "Captain wants to see you!"

I made my way aft, lurching this way and that, clinging to whatever was handy, dreading the captain, wishing I'd had time to shed some of my clothes. I wore six layers and could hardly move. Hard bread and salt beef bulged in my pockets beneath my oilskins.

"Going somewhere?" Briggs said, grinning as I passed him. They were the first words he'd spoken to me since he'd been tarred. "Say hello to your ladylove." I ignored him, hating his smug, ugly face, and continued aft.

Light from the binnacle lamp illuminated Thorndike's face beneath his sou'wester. Ice frosted his beard, and for a moment, while he peered at the compass, I saw the scar. The intensity in his eyes. My mouth went dry at the sight of him, my tongue a block of wood.

He looked up and saw me. "Robbins?"

"Aye, sir."

"Follow me."

Sleet stung my face as I followed him to the steerage companionway. Water swirled about my ankles, icy cold. *What does the captain want with me below?*

Holding a lantern aloft, Thorndike clambered down the companionway. I took a deep breath and followed, wishing I could hide in my bunk instead.

We were in the blubber room. Aft of the companionway was the door leading to steerage. Save for the blubber pieces held in pens to prevent them from sliding round, the blubber room was empty. Wasting no time, the captain proceeded down the hatchway and into the hold. Huge casks lined the floor, wedged in side by side. The *Sea Hawk* moaned and shrieked even louder in the hold, as if the ship were alive and suffering. A shiver trickled down my spine like ice water.

The captain hung the lantern on a peg, snow and ice dripping from his sou'wester and oilskins.

Why would the captain bring me into the hold alone? My pulse roared in my ears, for I knew something terrible, right terrible, was about to happen.

Without a word the old man took hold of my arm and yanked me forward. As I stumbled over the casks, I wondered if I should resist. Refuse to cooperate. Turn back. He stopped beside one of the deck stanchions—wooden support posts ranging fore and aft down the center of the hold—stooped down, and grasped hold of a heavy chain lying there. It was round six feet long, with a shackle on each end. Thorndike fastened a shackle onto my wrist.

"Captain—what—what—"

And while I stood there stammering like a dummy, he wrapped the chain round the post and shackled the other end to my other wrist. By fire, I was chained to the post!

"Captain, why are you doing this? Please—you must let me go!" I pulled against the chain, the cold metal of the shackles biting my wrists. Panic fluttered in my chest.

Thorndike said nothing. He walked back over the casks, lifted the lantern off the peg, and began to climb the hatchway ladder. But before he climbed entirely out of the hatchway, he dug in his coat pocket, withdrew a packet, and flung it at my feet.

Elizabeth's letters.

"I'll deal with ye later," he growled as he left the hold and closed the hatch, plunging me into total darkness.

CHAPTER 12

"No! Please! Let me go! I haven't done anything wrong!"

I screamed for hours, it seemed. Finally, my voice hoarse, I collapsed. *It's useless. No one can hear me. No one knows where I am except Thorndike. If the ship wrecks now, I'm dead.* For the first time in my life, I could taste raw fear.

"I don't want to die," I sobbed. "I want to go home. I want to row to Palmer's Island with Dexter. I want to see Aunt Agatha again. And Elizabeth."

Elizabeth . . . I imagined her locked in her cabin. I imagined her terror as the storm raged.

For a long time I lay against the post, the wood rough against my cheek, until I noticed something was different. Something had changed. We were tacking. Tacking, in such seas and such wind? We'd normally wear ship, unless . . . unless . . . *we were near to running aground!*

I stood and strained against the chain, ignoring the pain shooting up my arms. "Down here! I'm chained in the hold! Help me! Someone, please—"

With a sudden boom, something scraped hard across the *Sea Hawk's* bottom. The ship heeled sharply to her side, knocking me off my feet. I screamed. At the same time, I heard an ear-splitting crack, felt a jab of splinters near my cheek. The *Sea Hawk* shuddered from stem to stern as timbers cracked and splintered and the deck buckled. *We've hit! We've hit! We're going down!*

Seawater roared into the hold.

Again I pulled against the chain. To my surprise, it whapped me in the face. *I'm free! The post must have broken!* Already the water was past my ankles, my feet numb with cold. I staggered toward what I believed was the direction of the hatchway ladder. Still shackled to my wrists, the chain clanked against my shins.

I stumbled over casks, hands in front of me in the pitch black, everything out of kilter, lopsided. *Where is the ladder? Oh God, where is it?* I turned round and round, this way, that way, as water rushed past my knees, my thighs, my hips, then my waist. The freezing water sucked my breath away, shriveled my insides.

God help me!

Suddenly, a huge wave hit the *Sea Hawk* and crashed through the hold. It swept me off my feet and tossed me against the hatchway ladder as if I were no more than a fly under a fly-swatter. The chain smashed me across the bridge of my nose. I gulped blood and salt water and whale oil, unable to breathe. My brain withered in the icy cold. My muscles clenched in pain. My lungs wanted to explode. Panic flooded my veins, while my mind screamed, *This is the end!* With a will, I forced the panic back, forced myself to think, *think!*

Before I could be swept away, I flung an arm over a step and began to climb. Blackness seeped through my mind, different from the pitch dark of the hold. I fought the blackness, fought the churning water as I pulled myself up step by step. Finally, with a great gasp of air, I collapsed on the floor of the blubber room, coughing, sucking in air. *I'm alive! I'm alive!*

After a moment of joyous celebration, thanking God, the angels, the stars, my father, Aunt Agatha, and everyone who had ever been nice to me, I dragged myself to my feet. There wasn't much time. Judging by the tilt of the deck, the *Sea Hawk* rested on the shore or on a shoal. But I knew she could be swept off at any minute and sink. Though it was still black as blindness, now that I had climbed the hatchway, I knew what direction I faced. I took a deep breath and lurched toward steerage, stooping so as not to bang my head on the overhead beams.

"Help! Down here in the blubber room! It's me, Nick!" I stumbled over something and fell headlong. It was hard, yet squishy and slimy. A blubber piece. I crawled along, over and around the blubber, mush oozing under my hands and knees.

Finally, I found the bulkhead and tumbled through the doorway just as the *Sea Hawk* gave a mighty groan and lurch. My heart near stopped ticking. *If she sinks now, I'm a goner.* I scrambled to my feet and fumbled my way through steerage. Through the far doorway, I could see a lantern burning low, hanging from an overhead beam in the officers' mess. I entered the room—still smelling of coffee and fried potatoes—and, with a clank of chain, removed the lantern from its hook. Turning up the wick so that it burned bright, I edged past a table built round the mizzen and into the captain's cabin.

"Elizabeth!" I banged on her door.

"Nicholas! Oh, Nicholas! Get me out of here!" I heard fear in her voice and knew she'd been crying.

The door was locked tight. "Stand back! I'm going to bust down the door!" I hung the lantern overhead. Grasping the chain, I swung back and hit the door as hard as I could. Wood splintered.

"Hurry!"

Again I hit the door. Again. Swinging the chain was about as easy as swinging an anchor. Again. Again. Finally, with a crack, the door splintered in half. I ripped it away with my bare hands, amazed at my strength.

Elizabeth squeezed through the opening. She wore her hooded reindeer coat belted round the waist, deerskin trousers, and sealskin boots. Her eyes were bloodshot and watery. Her chin trembled. "I'm ready."

I wanted to hug her but instead grabbed the lantern and her mittened hand. "Follow me!" I stumbled up the companionway, tripping over my chain once, twice, hearing her ragged breathing behind me.

Out we staggered onto the sloping deck. Cold hit me like a sledgehammer, knocking my breath away. I was sopping wet, bareheaded—my woolen cap and sou'wester lost in the hold. I held up the lantern. Chain rattled. Needles of thick snow stabbed my skin, swirled round the light like thousands of moths, hissing against the glass, stinging my eyes so that I had to squint to see. My breath came out in foggy gasps. From what I could tell, the *Sea Hawk* was deserted—masts down like felled trees, rigging tangled like a spider's web.

"Hello!" I shouted. "Anyone here?"

At first, all I heard was the howl of the wind, the groan of timber, and the ringing of the ship's bell as waves crashed in and over the ship. Then I heard a vague shouting.

"Over here!" Elizabeth tugged me down the slanted deck. "Hurry!"

We picked our way over rigging and broken spars and then peered over the rail.

Sheltered somewhat from the storm, a whaleboat lay in the lee of the wrecked *Sea Hawk*. In the center of the boat, clinging to the rope that kept it from being swept away, sat Dexter. His face was white and pinched with cold. When he saw us, a spark lit his eyes and his mouth flew open. "Jerusalem crickets, Nick! I thought you were dead! Miss Elizabeth—I thought you were with the captain!"

"Where are the others?" Elizabeth asked. "Where's my father?"

"Everyone's abandoned ship, took off in other whaleboats. Nick, I swear I looked for you everywhere. Where were you?"

"I'll explain later."

"Well, what are you two standing there for? I was about to shove off. Hurry! Climb down before it's too late!"

Elizabeth hesitated only a second before she clambered over the side. It was tricky, what with the wind screaming and the whaleboat rocking about like a seesaw. She finished the last few feet by falling flat on her back in the whaleboat.

"C'mon, Nick, hurry!" cried Dexter.

Just then, I heard a cry. A moan. It was human and coming from amidships. A chill raced over my scalp. *By fire, someone else is aboard!* "Hang on a while longer, Dex! I hear someone! I'll be right back!"

"Wait—Nick! Don't . . ."

I stumbled in the direction of the cry, the blasted chain knocking the devil out of my bruised shins. There! I heard it again! "Where are you?" I hollered.

Then I saw movement. I held up my lantern, squinting

through the blinding snow, the smell of burning whale oil sharp in my nose. Pinned under the mainmast was a man. Blood seeped out of his mouth. His lips moved. A hand twitched.

It was Captain Thorndike.

I stopped short.

Part of me wanted to run back to Elizabeth and Dexter. To pretend I'd never seen Thorndike pinned beneath the mast. I hated Thorndike. He deserved to die.

But part of me wouldn't let him die.

I don't know how long I stood there—only seconds, likely— but when Thorndike opened his eyes and I glimpsed the raw pain, the defeat, my hatred vanished. *Hatred.* One second it was there; the next second, gone. Swallowed in the heart of a storm.

I hurried over and set down the lantern.

He glanced at me, at the chain still dangling from my wrists. "Go," he said, his voice raspy and weak. "Take Elizabeth and go while you can. Leave me."

I didn't answer. There wasn't time. I looped my chain round the back of my neck so it wouldn't clank against my shins, wishing I'd thought of it earlier, grabbed him under the arms, and pulled. The mast wasn't pinning him entirely, for it rested on the bulwarks, leaving a gap above the deck. I pulled again, straining, blood surging in my head.

"Go! 'Tis an order! Save Elizabeth. I beg of ye. Go after the *Merimont* while there's time. The *Sea Hawk* won't stay afloat much longer."

I tried for a better grip. He stiffened with pain. Again I pulled. Nothing. He was wedged too tight. For a moment I considered leaving him as he'd ordered, knowing that Elizabeth and Dexter were waiting for me, that they'd never leave without me. But no sooner did I think it than I was pulling again.

Suddenly, the *Sea Hawk* lurched to starboard. The mainmast groaned and shifted. Thorndike was free!

"C'mon, sir! Can you walk?"

Hanging on to the mainmast, Thorndike staggered to his feet. He winced and gasped.

I placed his arm round my shoulder, grabbed my lantern, and off we went, stumbling over rigging and debris. A crate of potatoes. A cage filled with straw, feed, and dead chickens. A broken oar. A scrap of sail. Blubber. Ninny, struggling against her rope, hooves scrabbling on the slanted deck, bleating, looking at me with frantic eyes.

Thorndike and I peered over the rail.

Dexter and Elizabeth sat in the boat, facing us. Elizabeth gasped, "Father! I—I thought you were gone!" Her voice broke. "I—I thought you'd left me!"

"Hurry!" cried Dexter. "Captain Thorndike, sir, climb down! Quickly!"

While Thorndike climbed down, I scrambled back to fetch Ninny. "Good girl. Steady now, steady. Don't be frightened." By the time I returned with the goat, Thorndike was in the boat. After lowering the lantern, I slung Ninny over my shoulders and down I went. She struggled, blasting my face with hot goat breath and poking my cheek with a horn. Finally, with a grunt, a bleat, and a clatter of chain and hooves, we were in. Elizabeth took hold of Ninny.

"Grab an oar, Nick, let's go!" Dexter cast off our moorings, and we were off. "Pull! Pull!"

No sooner were we away than the *Sea Hawk* lurched and groaned. With a sigh, her bell still ringing, she rolled over and sank beneath the waves.

CHAPTER 13

*W*e checked the compass, set our sail, and headed southwest.

Thorndike unlocked my shackles. I was about to toss the chain overboard when he stopped me. "Keep it. We might need it." He collapsed in the center of the boat, saying nothing more, clenching his jaw whenever he trimmed the sail. Elizabeth cast worried looks at her father but had no time to tend to him, for she had tied Ninny to the mast and now bailed frantically.

Dexter sat at the bow holding the lantern, looking ahead, snow swirling round him in gusts. I sat at the stern operating the tiller according to Dexter's commands. "Ice four points off the starboard bow!" "Keep her off a point!" "Ease her!"

"Luff a little!" "Brace yourselves, here comes a big one!" "Steady as she goes!"

Captain Thorndike was injured—how badly I didn't know. And me—beneath my stiffened oilskins, my woolen clothes seemed turned to ice. The wind seeped through the seams, through the very fabric. I shivered violently, muscles rigid, eyes watering, face stinging and numb, as salt spray lashed me.

I thought my teeth would freeze off as the wind continued to blast out of the northwest. The night thickened, the black, heavy sky seeming within reach of my fingers. Ice, ghostly and thick, coated the weather side of the boat, the rigging, the mast.

"I can only see a few feet, sir!" Dexter yelled over the scream of the wind. "We're sailing blind!"

Thorndike stirred and pointed south. "Put in to shore, Nicholas."

"Sir?" My teeth chattered.

"The risk of stoving our boat is too great! We must stop for the night."

Dexter gaped at him. "But the pack ice, sir. If it reaches us before we can sail through the channel, we'll be trapped. We've got to catch the *Merimont*! It's our only hope!"

Suddenly, our whaleboat bumped something hard. Dexter peered over the side, lantern in hand. "By fire, it's a ship's yard, sir! There's grommets, and a sail still attached."

Elizabeth stopped bailing. "But why would a ship's yard be out here? We're too far from the *Sea Hawk*'s wreckage for it to be hers."

Thorndike looked at me, his face stricken. Again I saw the defeat in his eyes. "Put in to shore, Nicholas."

Debris littered the beach, piled ten feet high. Timbers. Yards. Rope. Canvas, torn and ragged. Casks lying hither and yon, both broken and whole. A body, waterlogged and spongy white.

Elizabeth clamped a lace handkerchief over her mouth, eyes wide with horror.

Aye, it was wreckage. But not wreckage from the *Sea Hawk*. It was the *Merimont*.

"She must have wrecked." Dexter raised his lantern and looked out to sea. "Struck ice, probably."

"Smashed to bits," I said, my teeth clacking.

"Hello!" cried Thorndike. "Anybody here? Hello!" But no one answered. We were alone.

We unloaded the whaleboat and moored her as best we could to the debris. The whaleboat was too heavy for the four of us to drag onto the beach, Thorndike being injured, and me so freezing I couldn't grasp a rope.

We rolled the smaller casks up the black-pebbled beach, up and over snowy dunes, far away from the thundering waves. We set them upright in a tight rectangle, leaving a two-cask space on the lee for getting in and out. Over the top and sides of the casks we secured canvas, every scrap we could find, leaving one for the floor of our shelter. I thought I'd die before we finished. I kept falling. My hands couldn't grasp anything. Thorndike himself stumbled, falling to his knees, groaning.

Truly, we made a sorry spectacle.

We crawled into our shelter, the canvas beneath us stiff and crackling. While I drew my legs to my chest, shivering, Dexter opened the watertight lantern-keg that all whaleboats carried. Inside were matches, flint and steel, tinder, candles, tobacco, hard bread, and other such necessities.

Soon there was a fire going just inside the entrance to our shelter. Smoke wisped out the shelter and into the storm. Dexter tied Ninny outside near the fire with a half cask turned on its side as shelter; then he and Elizabeth left to find more firewood. Meanwhile, Thorndike collapsed at one end of our shelter, wheezing, lips bubbling with blood. I pulled off my brogans and draped my socks over one of the casks to dry, setting my brogans beside the fire. Bare feet toward the flames, knees to my chin, I rubbed my hands together over the fire, my teeth chattering, my body shaking uncontrollably.

"Nicholas."

At first I didn't hear him.

"Nicholas."

"S-sir?"

Thorndike lay flat on his back. His coat had fallen away, and I saw the gleam of the pistol, orange in the firelight.

"Take care of Elizabeth," Thorndike was saying, his teeth stained crimson.

"Sir?"

"Take care of Elizabeth. Please."

"What do you mean?"

"Sail hard first thing in the morning. 'Tis your only chance."

"But sir, you're coming with us."

He moaned and turned away. For a long time he said nothing, just wheezing. I told him to come sit at the fire, to warm himself, but I don't think he heard me. Then, his voice a gurgling whisper beneath the storm, "She's lost. . . ."

"Sir?" I said.

"I've failed . . . failed everyone. Should have gone down with her. Aye, should have gone down. It'd be done by now. Ah, Catharine! Catharine! To such depths have I sunk. . . ." He sighed, and my face warmed, for I knew I wasn't meant to hear this.

Finally, to my relief, Dexter and Elizabeth returned.

"Here." To my surprise, Dexter handed me my reindeer fur. "Sorry, but I took it." He grinned. "Thought you were dead, you know. Thought I was on my own."

I tried to smile, but my face wouldn't let me. "I—I'm glad you took it. I'd want you to have it."

"Take off your clothes and wrap yourself in the fur. It's dry. I hid it in the aft cuddy, away from the spray."

I glanced at Elizabeth, seeing color spread across her face before she looked away. Heat sprang to the roots of my hair. While she knelt next to her father, I fumbled with the buttons on my oilskin. "Dexter?"

"Aye?"

"Thanks—thanks for t-trying to find me," I stammered, my tongue thick with cold. "Thanks for staying behind after everyone else had left. Y-you're a true brother, D-dex."

Dexter shrugged and began to unbutton my oilskin coat. His hands shivered too, and he could hardly grasp the buttons.

By the time I'd wrapped myself in the reindeer fur, Dexter had wrung out my wet clothes and hung them over the casks nearest the fire. It was the last thing I saw before I fell into a shivering sleep.

I opened my eyes. Something was wrong.

I lay for a moment, my mind still groggy, until gradually I realized what it was. It was silent. The wind. The crashing of the waves. Everything silent.

I sat up. Dexter was gone. The early-morning air was crisp as crystals, smoky. My breath steamed. The fire burned. Flames snapped and curled. Dexter must have added wood. On the other side of the shelter, I saw the vague shapes of Elizabeth and Thorndike, huddled together.

Quiet as I could, I got dressed. My clothes weren't much drier than before—more like frosty and damp rather than freezing and soggy. I coughed out a lungful of smoke and broke out in a shiver, my nose, ears, and hands stinging with cold.

I pulled on my socks and brogans, thinking Dexter was likely loading the whaleboat with provisions, preparing to launch. We had to sail all day, I knew, and every day after until we met up with the whaling fleet before it headed south for the winter. Without a wind, and with about eleven hours of daylight, it would be a long day at the oar. That would warm my hands, all right. I crawled round the fire and out the shelter. I stood, stretched, and yawned, blinded in the brightness, wishing I were already home in New Bedford. Safe and snug.

The land stretched away from the shelter in an endless, barren, snow-covered plain. As far as I could see, there was nothing. Just ground to walk on and a few scrubby grasses poking up. It was a boring place to be, and seeing it made me anxious to be on our way. After relieving myself, I found Dexter standing at the shore atop one of the dunes.

"Morning, Dex."

Dexter said nothing, just pointed out to sea.

I blinked in disbelief, my smile slipping to my brogans.

A half mile offshore stood the pack ice. Old ice it was, snow-covered, jumbled in piles of pressure ridges like buildings tossed about in an earthquake. Between the pack ice and the shore, slush covered the water. "We're stuck," said Dexter grimly. "It's over."

CHAPTER
14

$\mathcal{T}$he weather turned bitter cold and the slush thickened into ice.

The first day, Dexter and I set about establishing camp. Thorndike lay inside the shelter, covered with the fur, wheezing, coughing up blood as Elizabeth tended him, her handkerchief soaked crimson. I wished I could do something for him.

For the time being, Dexter and I dragged the dead sailor behind a dune. Then we brought supplies up from the beach and stacked them round our shelter. Timber. Casks filled with tools, wood shooks for building more casks, sailcloth, tobacco, water, coal, tar, whalecraft, whale oil, and navigational equipment, including a sextant. Dexter joked that at least now we'd know where we were stuck. We removed the canvas from atop our shelter and reinforced the roof with timbers laid over the rectangle of barrels. We then secured the canvas back over the rafters and down the sides of the barrels with rope. Rigging a set of block and tackle, we hauled the whaleboat off the beach and placed her upside down next to our shelter. Underneath we stowed what food supplies we'd found—a keg each of tea and grog, plus three kegs filled with hard bread. (The bread inside a fourth keg was ruined, soaked in seawater.) For all our searching we never did find a cask of salt beef or pork. Three kegs of hard bread and Ninny's milk had to last us through the winter. We figured how much hard bread each of us could eat per day—round half a pound—and began to ration.

A few days later, after I thought we'd combed the beach for everything of value, I found a good-sized tin of pickled meat. I foolishly picked it up with a wet, frozen hand, too late feeling the sizzle of cold. The skin on my thumb pad tore off, stuck bloodless to the tin.

Despite my skinless thumb and the blood blisters that formed on my fingers, we made a great ceremony of supper, spreading pickled meat atop our hard bread. We opened our one keg of grog and warmed ourselves from the inside out. Even Thorndike seemed to revive, sitting up a bit. For the first time since the shipwreck, Elizabeth looked happy. Dexter told lots of jokes that evening, and we busted our sides laughing. More than once, I turned to see Thorndike watching me as I laughed with Elizabeth. Once he saw her grasp my hand and smile at me warmly. I tensed, expecting him to order her away from me, but he looked away and said nothing.

Elizabeth made a blubber lamp out of the empty tin of meat, using strips of sailcloth as the wick. It was ingenious, I thought, and told her so. Now we had two lanterns and our little shelter shone with white light, though it was still dim and sometimes smoky if the wicks weren't trimmed proper or if the lantern glass turned sooty. The bloodless skin on the meat tin withered, cooked, and finally fell off.

We had plenty of wood to last us through the winter, what with the wreckage, and wood smoke swirled through our shelter and our lungs, making us squint and our eyes water. Dexter cut a hole in the top of the canvas, and that helped, but the smell and taste of smoke never went away. We started to look like dark-skinned Gypsies.

Outside the shelter, snow glittered like millions of diamonds, every surface coated with hoarfrost. Hoarfrost also lined the inside of our shelter, more than an inch thick. If we accidentally touched the canvas, a shower of prickly ice rained down, onto our necks, into our hair. If we built up the fire too much, the hoarfrost lining melted, making a soggy, dripping mess, our breath a foggy dew that seeped through everything and chilled us to the bone.

At night, color drenched the sky in strange swirling clouds— green, red, blue, purple. It was beautiful, like dancing flame. Dexter and I stood watching, our faces shimmering till our blood turned to slush and we dived back into the shelter.

Dexter and I buried the washed-up body some distance away, but not before I took the man's gloves, hat, clothes, and coat. I'd lost my gloves and hat on the night of the shipwreck. His was a nice thick woolen cap, knitted by his mother likely. The coat we used at night as an extra layer, having given the fur to Elizabeth and her father. I lay under the coat next to Dexter, wondering what had happened to all our shipmates. To Garret, Sweet, Cole, Walker, Briggs, Cook, Duff, and the others. Were they drowned like the fellow who'd owned this coat? Had they sailed ahead of us down the open lead, and were they now heading south through the Bering Strait toward the Sandwich Islands? Were they shipwrecked like us?

After a week of drinking tea and goat's milk, and eating only hard bread and one tin of meat, we were stricken with hunger.

"I need meat." Dexter knelt next to Elizabeth, rubbing his hands over the fire as she added more wood. "I swear I'll starve without it."

"Drink the oil," said Thorndike, wheezing.

We stared at the captain. "Drink the oil," he repeated. "'Tis edible and 'twill give us fat."

Following the captain's orders, we each drank a cup of whale oil. I expected to have to choke it down like pig slop, but it was surprisingly good. After this, we soaked our hard bread in oil. Along with Ninny's milk, it still wasn't enough, but I stopped feeling so weak and shaky.

During the day, Dexter and I went hunting. Armed with harpoons and blubber knives, we scouted round within sight of our camp, as stealthy as we knew how to be. But nothing moved. Nothing breathed. Nothing lived in this desert of ice. We came to realize that it really didn't snow much here. Truly, it was an Arctic desert. What snow there was, though, didn't melt, instead rising and swirling in a blinding whiteness with every gust of wind.

Ten days after we'd come ashore (I cut notches daily in one of the casks), while I sawed wood into fire-sized pieces, Elizabeth approached. Her nose was pink and peeling, her skin chapped, dusted with soot. Shadows were stamped beneath her eyes like half-moons. Two yellow braids snaked out from her hood.

"I've never thanked you for saving my life."

I flushed, still sawing. "It's what any man would have done."

"But they didn't. You were the only one who stayed behind to help me."

"Dexter would have, if he'd known."

"Nick—" She paused.

"Aye."

"I want to go home."

I looked up from my sawing.

"I don't want to be here anymore," she continued, blinking back tears. "I wasn't meant to be here."

"None of us were."

"It's all a mistake." She brushed her mitten across her face, then looked straight at me with those cornflower-blue eyes, her chin quivering. "Are we going to get out of here? Alive, I mean?"

I wanted to tell her everything would be fine, that a lead would open in the ice tomorrow, and then we'd be on our way to safety. That a seal would pop up and we'd have meat to eat. And blubber. But somehow that's not what came out. "No matter what happens, I'll never leave you."

She sniffed, fiddling with one of her braids, seeming to think about what I'd just said. What it meant. "I'm worried about my father."

"I know. Me too."

"What if he dies?"

"Don't think about it, Elizabeth. Just don't think about it. Brings bad luck, it does."

"First my brother, then my mother, then Prince Albert, and now my father. I hate the sea. It takes everything I love. *Everything.*" She turned away.

I set down my saw, turned her to face me, wrapping my arms round her. I put my cheek against hers, patting her back, as if that would somehow whisk us home to New Bedford.

"I'm scared, Nicholas."

"Me too."

We stood there a long time, arms wrapped round each other. Pressed cheek to cheek. I thought, *If everything can stay like it is right now, we'll be all right.*

But of course, nothing stays like it is.

I know that now.

I had a terrible singing voice, but sing I did. Dexter lay on his back staring into nothing. Elizabeth fingered her ivory figure of Prince Albert and looked a million miles away. Thorndike, his face tanned and weather-worn, simply watched Elizabeth as if he'd never seen her before and was trying to figure out who she was. We'd just eaten our meager meal of hard bread, whale oil, and goat's milk.

This place could use some cheering, I figured, and so, without another thought, I started singing, loud and off-key. They all blinked in surprise. *"'Tis advertised in Boston, New York and Buffalo, five hundred brave Americans, a-whaling for to go, singing . . ."* I stopped, frowning. "What are you waiting for? C'mon, join in."

Dexter rolled his eyes but started singing: *"Blow, ye winds in the morning, and blow, ye winds, high-igh! Clear away your running gear, and blow, ye winds, high-o! They send you to New Bedford, that famous whaling port, And give you to some land sharks to board and fit you out. . . ."*

Meanwhile, Elizabeth came and sat next to me, smiling as she began to sing. *"The skipper's on the quarterdeck a-squinting at the sails, When up aloft the lookout sights a school of whales. 'Now clear away the boats, my boys, and after him we'll travel, But if you get too near his fluke, he'll kick you to the devil!' . . .* C'mon, Father, sing like you used to! Remember? When I used to play the piano?"

I caught the expression on Thorndike's face. It was that same look of defeat I'd seen in his eyes when he lay under the mainmast. Raw pain. One by one, beginning with mine, our voices trailed off into silence. Thorndike turned away.

The rest of us exchanged looks. Dexter shrugged, ran a hand through his hair, pulled his cap on tight, and rolled over as if to go to sleep. Elizabeth gazed at her father, placed her carving of Prince Albert in her pocket, and lay down too. I sighed, my attempt at cheering folks smashed all to heck. I stoked the fire, blew out the oil lamp, and lay down beside Dexter.

That night, the clouds moved in and the wind started to blow again. Outside the shelter, Ninny bleated. And bleated.

I heard Elizabeth get up. Heard a rustle of clothing. Then she was past me and out the entrance. "Hush, Ninny," she said.

She fumbled with the lantern. The night outside our shelter suddenly brightened. Her shadow moved away. She got up every night to do her necessary business. Although she didn't know it, I always stayed awake to make certain she came back.

After the crunch of her footsteps faded away, there was nothing. Just the wind. And Ninny bleating. Tugging on her rope.

Sleep pressed down, heavy and warm. I reached up and pinched my tongue between my fingernails to keep me awake. I suppose a needle poked in my eye would have felt just as good.

A scream shattered the night.

I sat up, my scalp prickling. I heard a snuffle. Then a horrible, animal grunt.

Without waiting for Dexter, I raced out of the shelter. "Elizabeth!" I shouted, grabbing a blubber knife from our pile of supplies.

Another scream.

Then a roar.

It's coming from the shore! My God! I raced toward the beach, scarcely aware that my feet were bare. The lantern sat on the beach. In its illumination, I saw a flash of yellowish white fur. A ripple of muscle. Claws longer than my fingers. My heart leapt to my throat. *A bear! Blood and thunder! A polar bear!*

Elizabeth lay on her back in front of it, her knees drawn up, kicking wildly at the bear, shrieking, shrieking, as it swiped at her.

"Elizabeth!" I raced toward the white mass, screaming at the top of my lungs, my blubber knife out in front of me, terror bubbling like ocean froth.

The bear lifted its head. It swung toward me and stared with small black eyes. In an instant, the bear charged. I saw a gaping mouth. A black nose. A pink tongue. Fangs. Heard the pounding of its feet. Its claws scrabbling the stony beach. The huff of its breath.

My God!

"Down, Nicholas! I'm going to shoot!" Thorndike's voice!

I threw myself flat on my face, stones stinging my chin. My knife clattered away, I don't know where.

And in that second I heard the most horrible sound: the click of a gun that won't fire.

Click.

Click.

Then the bear was on me.

I felt teeth in my scalp.

Hot breath on my neck.

Liquid slipping down my cheeks.

I knew I was screaming, thrashing; I could hear it. But it sounded like a stranger, as if the screams really didn't belong to me, as if the boy lying crunched beneath a polar bear were someone else.

I heard others screaming.

Elizabeth. Thorndike. Dexter.

And then I was on my back, my knife in my hand again. I don't know when I rolled over, or even how, but I was on my back and fighting. Fighting for my life.

I slashed at the bear, catching it across the shoulder.

A huge wound opened.

Blood stained the fur. Spattered in my mouth, my eyes.

Claws. Fangs.

Screaming.

Then the bear was off me.

In a flash of white, he attacked someone else.

I lay for a moment, dazed, my head wet, then realized.

My God! The bear's attacking Thorndike!

And then I was on my feet. There was another blur of white. A deep-throated growl. A slash of claws.

Elizabeth screamed as Thorndike collapsed to the ground, his bones suddenly turned to jelly. At the same time, I swung at the bear with my knife. Another wound.

With a grunt the bear looked at me, turned, and ran. In a heartbeat, it seemed, he was gone. Lumbering down the beach.

We huddled in our shelter. Lantern light glowed behind the smoky glass. At the entrance, the fire blazed and snapped, stoked to ward off the bear. Smoke whisked round the shelter and out the hole above. Hoarfrost melted and dripped. Ninny was silent.

"I'm dying," Thorndike said, his voice near lost in the howl of the wind and the snap of canvas. He sat propped against a cask, his arms hanging limply at his sides. Half his scalp was torn away. Blood trickled down his face, down his scar, and into his beard.

Elizabeth mopped his face with her stained, tattered handkerchief, then laid her head against his chest and wrapped her arms round him. "You can't go, Father. Not yet. Please. I need you." Elizabeth had suffered gashes on her legs. For now, though, the bleeding had stopped. We would tend to her wounds, mine as well, in a moment. Not yet . . .

Thorndike caressed Elizabeth's face, his hand dark against her skin. "I'm sorry, daughter, for the pain I've caused ye. Sorry I blamed ye for your mother's death. Sorry for all I've done. You were right. I've been a poor father. Forgive me."

Elizabeth's face contorted. "I know you've only wanted good for me. I know that. Just don't die, please don't die! I—I love you, Father! I always have." She buried her face in his chest as he stroked her hair. Her shoulders heaved. My eyes stung with tears and I looked away.

"Nicholas, Dexter, take care of her. Bring her home, I beg of ye. The whaling fleet will come again this summer." Thorndike paused, his breathing labored. Each breath, slower, slower. "Find them. Travel south to them if ye must."

I nodded, unable to answer, wiping my nose on the back of my sleeve.

Dexter replied, "Aye, sir."

Overhead, the wind gusted and the canvas flapped against the rafters. Ice crystals rained down in a shower of white dust.

"You've been good boys. I'm sorry for all the misery I've caused ye. I misjudged ye, Nicholas, I see that now. Any captain would be proud to have ye for a son. Please—please take care of her. You're her only chance."

I heard Thorndike breathe again. And again.

Then, nothing. Just the wind. Elizabeth sobbing.

I pressed my face into my hands, the terrible truth wrapping round me.

Thorndike was dead.

Elizabeth's injuries weren't so terrible, considering. She had four deep gashes on her left thigh, one near five inches long. There were other gashes too, some on her arms, but the ones on her thigh were the worst. I stitched her gashes together the way Thorndike had told me before he died. In the casks storing sail-cloth were needles for mending sails. The needle was so cold it blistered my fingers as if it were red-hot. After warming the needle over the fire, I threaded it with a strand of hemp and went to work.

Elizabeth was most brave, what with only a few swigs of grog to dull the pain and a needle big enough to stitch an elephant. Not to mention her father's body lying nearby, covered with a sailcloth. Fat tears rolled down her cheeks, but she never made a sound. After her wounds were treated, Elizabeth turned silently away from us.

Then it was my turn.

Dexter inspected my head, said I had a fat blubber-head, and it was no wonder the bear couldn't get a good grip. Said my thick woolen cap had saved me. Only a few gashes here and there, and only one was deep enough to maybe take a peek at my brains, which wouldn't be much to look at anyways. The liquid all over my face was mostly bear slobber. I knew Dexter was trying to be funny so Elizabeth would laugh, for he kept making jokes and glancing at her. But she said nothing. Dexter looked at me, his brown eyes mirroring my concern. He added a few stitches to my big gash, ordering me to stop blubbering like a blasted baby and saying he knew it didn't hurt any more than sticking your foot in a sausage grinder.

By the time Dexter finished, morning was near. We lay down next to Elizabeth. But I know no one slept. I heard their silence, because the same silence was inside of me.

It was the silence of listening.

Listening for Ninny to bleat.

Listening for a grunt. A huff. The scrape of claws on sandy gravel.

But we heard nothing. Nothing but the wind. The snap of fire. And the silent heaviness of death.

I hacked at the frozen earth with a broken harpoon. I heard the sound of my breathing—ragged and gasping. Sweat drenched me. Beside me, Dexter used a crowbar. For a long time, neither of us spoke. We just chopped and hacked. Chopped and hacked.

"It's deep enough," said Dexter finally.

It wasn't really deep enough—more of a slight depression than a grave—but I nodded. We had reached a layer of permafrost so frozen we could dig no deeper.

The body was stiff. We slid it into the hole. I stood for a moment, breathing hard, staring, then bent over and yanked off his boots. Seemed silly to waste good boots.

"His socks, too," said Dexter.

And his coat, his hat, his gloves . . . *God forgive us.*

After we covered the body with as much snow and tundra as we could scrape together, I began to pound the wooden marker into the ground. I'd spent all morning on it. It read:

Here lies Ebenezer Thorndike
Captain of the Sea Hawk
Killed by a bear
October 8, 1852

With a sharp crack, the marker splintered in half. I cursed and jammed the harpoon in its place, propping the marker against it.

We stepped back.

It was a crude and ugly grave. An arm stuck out, rigid, its fingers like claws. Bare feet poked out, frost forming on the toes.

"Rest in peace." I tried to think of something else to say. A prayer, maybe. It was too cold, though, and all I could think of was "Ashes to ashes. Dust to dust."

Dexter nodded. "Aye. Here lies Captain Thorndike forevermore."

As we turned away, back toward our shelter, the wind got to

howling. Snow peppered my eyes. Everything turned white. Sweat chilled me to my marrow.

Dexter and I crawled into our shelter, where Elizabeth lay, blood still crusting her hands and smeared across her cheek. I laid the coat over her. "Better?"

But instead of answering, she began to cry. As she cried, Dexter and I looked at each other, an unspoken understanding passing between us.

Now that Thorndike was dead, we were alone, terrible alone, in this vast wilderness. And unless a miracle happened, all of us would die.

Finally, days later, when the storm let up, I went to take care of Thorndike's grave. Dexter stayed behind in the shelter, for we never left Elizabeth alone.

I carried the blubber knife with me for protection. It was a good weapon, with a two-foot-long blade, sharp as a razor, used to cut apart blubber pieces. If it could hack a whale, I knew it could hack a bear. It already had—twice—which was likely why the bear hadn't returned.

A drift of snow had settled against the body on the windward side. To leeward, I saw an arm, a foot, white with ice. Using the bail bucket from the whaleboat, I scooped up gravel from the beach and hauled it overland to where we'd buried him. It took me three hours. I piled it deep so that the bear wouldn't smell him, all the while looking round me, gripping my knife so hard my knuckles popped.

The next day I visited the dead sailor's grave, intending to tidy it up. I wish I hadn't. The body was dragged from the grave, half eaten. I'd never seen the insides of a human body before. I ran, leaving my hard bread behind, a steaming little pile in the snow.

At least we now had two extra coats, extra wool sweaters and trousers, a reindeer fur, and extra gloves, hats, and boots. And when we all slept together at night under the fur, huddled close for warmth, it was sometimes bearable.

My stomach hurt all the time now. Growling, empty, gnawing. All we'd had to eat for the three weeks we'd been shipwrecked were hard bread, milk, and whale oil. Of water we had all we could want. We melted snow in a metal dipper over the fire. The whale oil, much as we needed it, had its drawbacks. It turned our bowels to soup. It was hard to figure what was more miserable—starving to death, or whipping down my drawers in the freezing cold ten times a day so I could drain my insides.

Much of the time, when either Dexter or I wasn't pretending to hunt, we stayed in the shelter. Elizabeth sewed clothing from sailcloth. I milked Ninny, keeping her half cask filled with fresh tundra grasses for warmth and food. When I wasn't milking Ninny or hunting, I whittled and carved wood. Dexter told jokes and kept the fire and lanterns going. He loved telling stories, too, spinning yarns that almost made me forget where we were. Almost. Elizabeth was silent most days, saying only what was necessary. There was a sadness in her eyes that never left now. I longed to take her sadness away, but nothing I said or did seemed to matter.

On the twenty-seventh day of October, I turned sixteen years old. Everyone forgot except me, even though I'd reminded them last week. I spent the day curled up, shivering, far away from the fire, wondering if Aunt Agatha had forgotten me too. It was a miserable day and I was glad when it was over.

The sun only stayed up for seven hours a day now, never high, skimming the horizon like a rock across a pond, bathing the sky in purples and pinks and drenching the ice in a bluish shimmer before heading back down. Even in the dark, even on moonless nights, it was possible to see, as the ice and snow seemed to gleam with lights of their own.

"I'm going hunting," said Dexter one day in early November.

I rubbed my hands over the fire, my stomach pinched even though I'd just eaten supper. "And you need my permission?"

"No, you don't understand. I mean, I'm going hunting. I'll be gone for a while."

I gaped at him. "Gone? What do you mean? What are you going to hunt? All we've seen is the bear."

Dexter brushed back a lock of sandy hair and gazed at me calmly.

My eyes widened. "Are you crazy?"

"Look, either he hunts us, or we hunt him."

"Either way, we lose. He'll kill you."

Dexter shrugged. "We can't survive on three casks of hard bread for the next seven months. One cask is half gone already, and besides, I'm so hungry I could eat a bear myself."

Elizabeth sat nearby, mending a rip in my coat. I knew she was listening, and silently cursed Dexter for discussing this in front of her.

"Or we could kill Ninny," Dexter suggested.

I'd dreaded this moment. I'd known it was coming. I had my speech prepared. "The meat would be gone in a few days. Right now, all we have to do is feed Ninny tundra grasses and she'll give us milk."

"She won't live through the winter. Her milk is getting thin, and there's not much of it."

I crossed my arms. "So we'll worry about that when the time comes. For now, hands off."

Dexter rolled his eyes. "You never could stand for anything to get hurt." He added another piece of wood to the fire. "Well, I guess that settles it, then. I'll leave in the morning."

"It settles nothing. You promised Aunt Agatha you'd bring me home. You promised Thorndike you'd take care of Elizabeth. So you see? You can't leave."

"What do you think I'm trying to do?" Dexter was raising his voice. "Blast it all, Nick, sometimes I swear you don't have a brain in your head. A bear would provide us meat for the winter and another fur besides. I'm trying to do what's best."

"I have a brain enough to know when you're being foolish."

"Foolish!" Now Dexter was practically screaming, his normally easygoing expression livid with anger. The only other time I'd seen him this mad was when I'd tossed his toy ship out the cupola window when we were little because he wouldn't let me play with it. "You want to hear *foolish*? How about a sailor who can't stay away from the captain's daughter? How about a sailor who doesn't know enough to burn her letters, and instead leaves them lying round for anyone to find? How about a sailor who can't stay at the helm during an emergency, or who can't remember port from starboard?"

"Fine. Go. I hope the bear eats you."

"Darn right I'll go. No one can stop me."

"I certainly won't."

The next day, nobody spoke as we outfitted Dexter for his journey. A harpoon. A canvas knapsack filled with hard bread. A blubber knife. Rope. For water, he'd have to eat snow or ice. Finally, when it came time, Dexter gazed out across the sea ice and in a tight voice promised to stay along the shore so he wouldn't get lost.

I said nothing, still so steamed I could fry an egg atop my head.

Then with a hail and farewell, he was gone.

CHAPTER 16

A week later, Dexter still hadn't returned.

Afraid he might be lost, during what daylight hours were left, I built a fire on two casks stacked one atop the other. Poised precariously on adjacent casks, breath white, I banged flint and steel together. A shower of sparks fell onto the tundra grasses, and as I blew, a thread of smoke curled up. I added more grasses, then small pieces of wood, and finally larger ones that I'd soaked in oil, until flames leapt and black smoke billowed.

I hurried down, choking on smoke and frozen stiff, rubbing my face and beating my hands so that sensation would return, a stinging ache that made me hop with pain. Every day I built this signal, accidentally tumbling off more than once in a cascade of sparks and casks that crunched the snowy gravel and near crushed me. I kept my blubber knife with me all the time. I glanced over my shoulder a thousand times a day.

Often I perched atop the casks, staring off into the whiteness while my signal fire burned. Long ago, pushed landward by the wind, the pack ice had reached the shore. Beyond the pressure ridges, torn and shattered, towering into the sky like blue teeth, the sea ice was flat, empty. Behind me, the barren plain stretched until land merged with sky. The beach, blanketed with gentle dunes, extended in each direction forever. An Arctic land filled with vast nothingness. *Where are you, Dexter? Can you see my fire? Do you know I'm sorry for what I said to you? I'm not angry anymore. Just come home.* I strained my eyes for movement. For a dark figure. Dragging a bearskin, piled high with meat.

He's dead. The bear ripped him to shreds and he's dead. With each day that passed, hope ebbed from me, swept away in a tide of despair. And in its place, like newly fallen snow, a terrible dread settled over my bones, cold and silent.

Every day I dragged Elizabeth out of the shelter and made her walk with me. I took Ninny with us, as if she were a dog and the three of us were on a Sunday stroll through New Bedford. We strolled to the shore. To the grave. Back to the shore. We picked over the debris lying on the beach as if we could find something of value this time, the hundredth time, something we couldn't see before. But we found nothing. And all the while I chattered like a magpie, trying to make up for Elizabeth's silence.

Meanwhile, Elizabeth continued to sew clothes from sail-cloth. Trousers, coats, oversized mittens to fit over our gloves. I sawed wood, kept the fire going, manned the signal fire, gathered tundra grasses, and milked Ninny. I also kept the blubber lanterns filled. It was sadly funny that we now had more whale oil than we could ever use or eat. At night I scarcely slept, listening to the wind moan and imagining footsteps, or claws scraping. Always I wondered where Dexter was, whether he was ever coming back, and whether I'd ever get to make up for the last words I'd spoken to him: *I hope the bear eats you.* Day after day those words haunted me. I lived them, ate them, breathed them, hated them.

One day I caught a glimpse of myself in the sextant mirror. I gave myself quite a fright because I looked like a waterfront tramp. A layer of filth covered me—soot, grime, and plain old dirt. Scrubbing my face with snow only seemed to rearrange matters.

I'd seen Aunt Agatha make soap once. She used whale oil and ashes and then did something to make it soap. Fine. If Aunt Agatha could make soap, so could I. I heated whale oil and ashes in the metal dipper. It boiled into a gray glop that didn't look or smell much like soap. After it cooled, I scrubbed my face with it. It was greasy and gluelike and I couldn't get it off. Now a layer of greasy slime glued my layer of soot, grime, and filth to my face.

At night, Elizabeth cried. She probably didn't think I could hear her, what with the wind moaning, but come the slightest noise I always snapped awake, reaching for my knife, wondering if Dexter had come home. I expect she cried for her mother and father, wishing she'd never heard of the *Sea Hawk* or Nick Robbins. I felt helpless. I heard Thorndike's voice saying, *Nicholas, Dexter, take care of her. Bring her home again, I beg of ye.* And now Dexter was gone, maybe dead. It was up to me.

One raw day when a heavy sky bore down and a chilling dampness penetrated my very bones, Elizabeth tossed aside her sewing and looked at me square. "I'm sick of sewing. I've always hated it." So saying, she set her jaw in a determined line, suddenly reminding me of her father.

I blinked with surprise. It was the first she'd spoken in weeks.

"Well, that's fine, I—I expect nine hundred pairs of canvas trousers and twenty thousand coats is plenty."

She rubbed her hands and put them over the fire. "What can I do now?"

"Well—uh—let me see—Ninny needs fresh tundra grass, and I was thinking of sawing wood for the fire."

"Fine." And out she went to work, leaving me with my jaw flapping.

Just like that, Elizabeth was talking again. We told each other all about ourselves, Elizabeth and I did. She told me that her father had taught her to play the piano, taught her Mozart and Beethoven—his favorites. She told me how she used to sneak into the lazaret, a storage area in the stern. How she'd have tea in the lazaret with her imaginary friends. How they'd play dominoes and talk about the weather and how they were all going to marry sea captains. How her mother used to make her a new dress every Christmas, but that now she supposed she wouldn't have a new dress even though they'd purchased material in Honolulu.

She looked away as she told me about Thomas, who'd died at sea. Everyone in her family had died at sea. She'd never marry a sailor, she vowed. She both loved and hated the sea.

I told her about my childhood, about Aunt Agatha and our considerable grand mansion, about my father and waiting for his ship, and his being smashed by a whale. I told her about my dreams, and how they were all wasted now, seeing as I didn't like the whaling life and was here in the Arctic besides.

"What will you do?" Elizabeth asked. She sat cross-legged next to me in the shelter, her face smudged with smoke.

I shrugged, fingering the wood I was carving. "Haven't considered it much." Suddenly, a thought came from somewheres deep inside. A happy thought that made me smile. "Why, I'll be a carver. Don't know why I didn't think of it before."

"A carver?"

"I'll carve figureheads for ships. I'll carve sea hawks and maidens—"

"King Neptune and mermaids!"

"Aye." I laughed, cutting another curl of wood off the block, feeling that a weight had been lifted from my shoulders. "I'll have my own shop downtown. I'll hang a sign out front. *Nicholas Robbins: Carver.*"

"I'll help you make the sign! It can say, *Nicholas Robbins: Extraordinary Carver.* Oh, Nicholas, you'll make a fine carver. The best around." She was quiet for a minute, watching me, then said, "Wait here." And to my surprise, she left the shelter.

I heard her digging not far away, wondered if I should go and keep watch, curiosity busting my britches. But before I could make up my mind, she returned, hiding something behind her back. "Guess what it is?"

"Hot gingersnaps."

"No."

"Soap."

She laughed. "We could use some, but no."

"A ship to take us home."

"No."

"I give up."

Eyes shining, she brought my whale's tooth out from behind her back.

"My tooth! Where did you find it?"

"I picked it up off the deck, you know, that night. I've been keeping it for you. I meant to give it to you when it was safe. On the night of the shipwreck, while I was still locked in my cabin, I stuffed it down my coat."

I wiped my eyes with the back of my glove, then took it from her gently. "I never thought I'd see it again. This is my father's ship, or *was* my father's ship. My father carved it."

"Talent must run in the family."

I set down the tooth and coughed, trying to hide the emotion in my voice. "So what are you going to do now?"

"What do you mean?"

I'd been intending to ask her this question for some time now but hadn't known how to approach it. Seemed a delicate subject, it did. "I mean, what are you going to do, now that your parents are—you know—"

A shadow passed over her face. "I've thought about it a lot. I—I don't really know. My father has a sister who lives in New York. I suppose I could go live with her, if she'll let me. But I've never met her."

"You could come live with Aunt Agatha and me," I blurted.

"Do you think she'd mind?"

I blew the chips away from the block and gazed at her. Now that I'd thought of it, it seemed a fine idea. "Aunt Agatha would be happy to have another woman round to keep her company, I expect."

"I—I could help with the housework. I could help with the garden, although I don't know how to grow anything. And maybe someday I'll go to school and learn to teach music. I've never been to a real school, with people my own age. I—I've given it some thought, Nicholas. I've got to make my own way, you know, just like you. And we could—you and I could—"

"What?"

She fiddled with her braids, twisting and curling them. Then, to my surprise, she leaned over and planted a kiss on my cheek. The kiss was warm, and I sat for a moment without moving, as if I'd turned into a figurehead myself. "I'd love to stay with you and your wonderful aunt," she whispered. Then she put both her hands on my cheeks and drew my face down to hers. I realized I was breathing hard.

She pressed her lips against mine. They were warm, so warm. The carving dropped to my lap. I felt myself kissing her back, pulling her close, felt her lips, her breath mixing with mine. *Should we be doing this? Here in the Arctic? With her father's grave so close?*

"Nicholas, what's wrong?" She pulled away, her forehead creased.

"Nothing. Nothing's wrong." I picked up my carving tool again, as if we'd merely had another walk to the beach, as if my heart weren't hammering like a cooper's mallet.

She turned away from me, silent, her jaw set.

Blast it all! I've gone and hurt her. Now she's not going to say anything for the rest of the winter! "You're a fine young lady, Miss Elizabeth. I'm proud to be here in the Arctic with you. Proud it's me, and not someone else. I figure you're the most special . . ."

But I'd ruined it. Our special moment. I'd ruined it, and no matter what I said after that, I could never make it up. She didn't speak to me as we lay down to sleep, blowing out the lantern and letting the darkness overtake us. All night she lay with her back to me.

In the morning when I awakened to the darkness, Elizabeth was burning with fever. "It's back," she whispered. "My sickness."

First the shipwreck. Then Thorndike dying. Then Dexter leaving. Now Elizabeth was sick again. If she died too . . .

Even the sun abandoned me. For the first time in my life, it refused to rise, instead fleeing south, leaving me stranded in the Arctic darkness. I don't know but what I'd never been more scared in my life. A right awful terror crawled into my chest and hunched there all the time now. I wished I could shove a stopper down my throat and not have to worry that it would come screaming out. But I was scared. So scared.

I soaked hard bread in whale oil and milk and fed it to Elizabeth. I put the mix of food in the dipper and kept it warm over the fire, or else it froze before I could get it to her mouth. If any of it dribbled down her cheek, I scraped it off and put it back in the dipper. Nothing could be wasted. Nothing. I cut a corner from my reindeer fur and boiled it. Then I cut it into bite-sized pieces, dipped one in oil, and ate it, hair and all. Surprisingly, it wasn't half bad. A little hairy, of course. Fact was, anything solid was better than nothing. I fed some to Elizabeth, and she ate it without complaint.

Sometimes she stared at me with eyes that seemed shrunken yet bulging at the same time, ringed with dark circles. Lips cracked and dry, she didn't just breathe, she panted. Chills often overtook her, and she shivered violently. When that happened, I held her in my arms. It was then the terror most wanted to come bursting out. Then, just as suddenly, she boiled with fever. Off came the hat. The mittens. The coat. But then she turned cold again. It never ended. And as I held her in my arms, I wished for the millionth time I had another chance to kiss her.

For five days a gale blistered out of the northwest. Three times the wind blasted the canvas covering from off the rectangle of casks, even though it was secured with rope and tucked beneath the heavy casks. Three times I ran after it, ice needles stabbing my face, my eyes watering.

By the time I placed the canvas back, taking an hour, two hours, the canvas whipping like a sail in a hurricane, Elizabeth had turned white, motionless. The fire and lantern had gone out. I always kept sulfur matches and tinder in the lantern-keg, and so got a fire going again, but each time I held my breath till I saw the flames.

Eating only a half pound of hard bread per day, plus whale oil, reindeer hide, and a little milk, I was so exhausted by the time I finished putting our shelter back together and building a fire and taking care of Elizabeth that every muscle shook and my knees trembled as though they belonged to someone who was ninety rather than sixteen. I lay beside her, panting, listening to the canvas snap and groan as snow flurries filtered through, dusting us with white.

When will this ever end?

Her fever.

The storm.

The forever night.

Dexter gone.

And I'm so hungry.

So alone.

Is it really going to end like this?

I figured it was the first of December or thereabouts when the wind stopped. While I had carved daily notches on a cask to mark the passage of time, sometimes I lost track of day and night what with storms, and the sun no longer rising. If my reckoning was correct, we'd been shipwrecked now for over two months, and Dexter had been gone near a month. I'd fed the last of the reindeer fur to Elizabeth the night before.

"Don't leave me," she begged when I said I was going to saw more wood for the fire. Her skin stretched across her jutting cheekbones, dusky with soot, her eyes small, frightened.

She's starving. The understanding stabbed me afresh. *She's starving and dying. We'll never make it out of here alive.*

I looked away and swallowed the lump in my throat. *What*

can we eat now? Ninny? "I won't be gone long. I'll keep watch on you the whole time. I promise." Sighing, I gently pried Elizabeth's hands off my arm. Lighting the tin lantern for her, I took the other lantern and my blubber knife and left the shelter.

Ninny crawled from her cask, hooves clattering, and bleated softly, shoving her head into my hand. My eyes smarted when I thought of having to kill her. For now I rubbed her between her horns, whispered that she was a good girl, the best, and then headed toward the shore, snow crunching beneath my boots. Ninny bleated after me.

The ground gleamed ghostly white beneath the blackest night. Stars glittered like ice crystals. Snow and hoarfrost covered the debris pile. Already the end of my nose and my cheeks were turning numb. I rubbed them briskly with the back of my glove to keep the blood flowing. I set down my lantern and knife and went to work, frigid air like glass in my lungs. It was deathly quiet, and every noise I made seemed unnaturally loud.

Usually I dragged large timber spars up beside the shelter, where I sawed them into smaller pieces. But after trying to drag the first spar, I realized I no longer had the strength. I would have to saw them on the beach and carry them piece by piece. Doing even the smallest job now took all my strength and will.

I fetched my saw and again set to work, only vaguely realizing that something was wrong. Something out of place. Different. I sawed for a while, until the realization seared me like the touch of frozen metal against bare skin.

Where the land met the shore ice, enormous tracks meandered along the beach. My skin erupted with goose bumps and I suddenly felt sick.

Bear tracks.

I whipped round, scanning every direction, heart crashing, blubber knife ready. I heard myself swallow. Every icy crag became a bear, every end of wood sticking out of the snow, a nose, as I slowly skirted the pile of debris. In the distance I heard Elizabeth cough.

Seeing nothing, I studied the tracks. It appeared the bear had stopped at the debris pile, investigated, but moved on. I followed the tracks down the beach for a ship's length, and they continued as far as I could see. The bear was gone.

Back to work I went.

Still, every fifteen seconds or so, I looked round me. Round the shelter, round the ice-covered sea, to the east and west, searching for movement. White against white. A black nose. I pricked my ears for the scrabble of claws. A huff of breath. After watching, listening, I went back to sawing. All I heard was the hum of the blade, my own loud breath, and Ninny bleating.

Bleating . . .

Bleating . . .

And as the hair raised on the back of my neck, I knew.

I was not alone.

CHAPTER 17

They came like phantoms.

Silent.

I saw them in the east, far away. Movement along the beach.

Nine of them.

Dragging a whaleboat behind them.

I waited, the terror inside of me thawing like ice under a warm sun. *They're here. Elizabeth and I are no longer alone. They've come. They're not dead after all. We'll spend the winter together. Maybe they have a plan for getting us out of here.*

Maybe they have food. Bear meat . . .

I recognized Dexter first, leading the way. I don't know when I started to run, but suddenly I was dropping my saw, running, stumbling over snow, ice, and gravel, with a strength I hadn't known I possessed. "Dexter!" I screamed.

Dexter dropped hold of the rope and ran too. "Nick! Thank God you're still alive!"

Then we were clapping each other on the shoulders, splitting our cheeks with grins. Others surrounded us. Garret, Sweet, Briggs, and more. Giddy with relief, I began laughing like a crazy man.

We're saved! We're saved!

Elizabeth's eyelids fluttered open. "Where were you?"

"They're here."

She looked at me with fever-reddened eyes.

"Sweet, Garret, Briggs—they're here! Dexter found them up the coast, close to where we shipwrecked. On the night of the storm, their boat got stove and they had to put in to shore. Then it iced over and they were stuck there like we've been stuck here. Of course, it isn't everyone—most folks didn't make it through the night of the storm, God rest their souls, but some did. Isn't that great? We're not alone."

"I'm thirsty."

I hardly paused for breath as I fetched her a drink from the dipper. "They're turning over their whaleboat now. They'll use it for a shelter. Dexter's helping them set up another shelter from our whaleboat."

Elizabeth closed her eyes and shivered. "I'm hungry."

"I'll fetch you some food, don't you worry. Everything's all right now. We're saved."

I practically skipped out of the shelter, so happy was I to have other people with me. "Garret!"

Garret was bent over, tying down a canvas. During the time he'd been in the Arctic, he'd grown a beard, scraggly and red. He'd also started chewing tobacco. As his beard froze from the condensation of his breath, he couldn't open his mouth wide enough to spit. Instead, he leaned over as juice dribbled out. His beard was now an amber icicle, growing longer each time he dribbled. "Hey, Bones," he said, opening his mouth with difficulty as ice crackled.

"Elizabeth's hungry. Fact is, we're both hungry. All we have is a little more than two kegs of hard bread left."

Garret stood and braced himself against the whaleboat. Clouds of breath steamed from him. He said nothing, couldn't talk really, panting as he was. Even in the darkness, his skin looked pale, and his freckles seemed frozen solid. His nose and cheeks were frostnipped, white and hard. I don't know why, but my scalp crawled as if it suddenly swarmed with bugs. "Garret, what's wrong?"

He blinked slowly. "Sorry, Nick, I thought you knowed. We don't got no food."

"But—I thought . . ." My voice trailed off and I turned away. I couldn't look at him anymore. *They're starving. Terrible starving. Worse than us.* Jutting cheekbones, hollowed eyes, shortened breath, all of it. I'd been blind not to see it before.

"All we had was the hard bread in the lantern-keg," Garret was saying. "Briggs 'pooned a seal once, but it didn't last long. We drank its blood first, and ate the skin too, fur and all. Another time, Sweet trapped a fox, but we ate it in a day. Couldn't keep the fellows off of it. Ate it like they was savages or something. I—I'm sorry, Nick, I'm just so—" Garret's voice faltered.

"What?"

To my surprise, he fell against the whaleboat and began to weep. Deep, wrenching, horrible sobs.

My blood turned to ice as the familiar terror clawed up my chest. "Garret, what is it? Tell me."

He shook his head, brushing his face on his sleeve. "It's just that I'm so tired of being *hungry*."

I patted his back, helpless, until he finally told me to go away and leave him be.

The sound of his crying trailed behind me as I stumbled back to the shelter. I lay next to Elizabeth. She was sleeping. I squeezed my eyes shut, teeth clenched, biting back the terror that swarmed inside of me like worms in a corpse.

Nothing to eat.

Nothing except a couple kegs of hard bread, divided between eleven people now instead of three.

At noon the next day, under a twilight sky, Henry Sweet, being the only mate who'd survived the shipwreck, called the crew together.

"I don't care what ye fetch," he told us, his black eyebrows powdered with ice and drawn together serious-like, fox cap snugged over his ears, "just so long as ye fetch it quick. Seals, bears, foxes—I even heard they have some kind of deer up here, though I ain't seen one. We've got weapons now that we didn't have before, so maybe we'll have better luck. Go two by two. Stay by the shore. Don't wander or ye'll be lost forever in this darkness. Bones, ye stay behind and look after Thorndike's daughter and keep the fire a-burning. Hopefully we'll be bring-ing ye a feast."

Briggs smirked. "Nick's a fine nursemaid, he is. Comes high recommended."

"Shut up, Briggs," snapped Dexter. "He's got far more nerve than you'll ever have. He fought off a bear when you'd've likely peed your pants."

"Boys! Boys!" Sweet held out stiffened arms between the two. "Don't be a-wasting your energies on fighting. We've all got to be thinking 'bout surviving. Our womenfolk at home need us to be calm. Now pick your hunting partner and be off with ye."

Twelve hours later, the last hunting party straggled back to camp. No one had caught anything. "We're whalemen," grumbled Briggs, flinging his harpoon aside, "not deer hunters."

A mask of ice weighing several pounds covered Garret's face. "I told Carrot Sticks not to chew tobacco," said Dexter, leading him into our shelter. "Told him beards only make things worse, but he wouldn't listen."

Garret couldn't talk, his mouth sealed in a muzzle of ice and tobacco juice. One eye peeped at us, the other frozen under the mask. We set him near the fire and chipped away at his face. After several hours, it was all off, and we finished the job by shaving his beard with a sheathing knife.

"Never again," said Garret, spitting out his wad of tobacco once he could move his mouth.

The next day Sweet sent everyone out again. And the day after that. And the day after that. Meanwhile, Garret's skin peeled off from his hairline to his Adam's apple. We joked and said we were having peeled carrots for supper, but somehow he didn't think that was funny.

Peeling your skin must be good luck, though, because the next day Garret and Dexter trapped several fat white hens with feathery legs. We made biscuit and fat white hen soup with milk. Though watery, it was delicious, and we made it stretch for a few days. But it didn't stop me from dreaming about custard pie and hot biscuits and fish chowder and the smell of flour on Aunt Agatha's hands.

One night I started awake, custard pie crumbling to ice in my mouth.

Something's wrong.

The blubber lamp was near out, the fire cold. A gray fog hovered near the ceiling. I glanced at Elizabeth, but she lay sleeping, her breathing steady. Dexter and Garret lay on the other side of her, both out to the world. Quietly, I pulled on my boots, lined with fat white hen feathers. Outside the shelter a sharp wind blew from the north. I pulled up my collar and yanked down my stocking cap, expecting to hear Ninny greet me. Instead, the wind moaned. Snow swirled round the ground in gusts.

I peered inside Ninny's half cask. "Here, girl."

The cask was empty.

I picked up Ninny's rope. It had been cut cleanly, as with a knife.

It was then I noticed a soft glow coming from the shore. Taking a deep breath, knowing what I would find but having to go anyways, I headed in that direction. Long before I arrived, I saw him.

Broad shoulders hunched over the fire, Briggs gnawed on a meaty shank, his pimply face glistening with grease. When he saw me, he stopped chewing.

"You killed her," I said, fists clenched.

He grinned and shrugged.

"You *stole* her! You didn't even let me say good-bye."

"Poor baby," he said with a sneer.

"And now you're hogging her all to yourself. You can't even see fit to share with your friends. You're a pig, Briggs. You hear me? A pig."

Briggs licked his fingers noisily and kept eating. "Shut up, Bones. I'm sick of you and your holier-than-thou ways. If 'twas up to you, we'd all die, we would. You're too stupid for your own good."

I choked back bile, hating his smug face covered with grease. I hated his easy smile, his arrogance. With a will, though, I closed my eyes and forced my fists to unclench. *Hatred never solves any-*

thing, I thought, remembering Captain Thorndike and how I'd once hated him. "I can't let you eat another bite." I opened my eyes, surprised my voice sounded so steady.

"Oh yeah? And what are you going to do about it, Bones? Eh, Bones? Gonna wrestle me for it?" Briggs smiled. "Tell you what. It'll be our secret. You and me. Why tell the others? I got some here just for you. Been saving it for you." He held up another meaty leg. When I didn't take it, his eyes narrowed. "You breathe one word about this, Bones, I swear, I'll—"

"Sure, I'll take it."

I could see the surprise on Briggs' face as I took the leg and sat beside him. After a moment, he grunted, shrugged, and tore off another bite.

"Say, we need some grog, don't we, Briggs? I can't eat goat without grog."

"Huh?"

"Wouldn't you like some grog to warm you?"

"I like grog."

"Why don't I sing for some grog?"

"Huh?"

I began to sing. *"It's all for me grog, me jolly, jolly grog, all gone for beer and tobacco! Spent all me tin on the lassies drinking gin, and across the western ocean I must wander!"*

Briggs stared at me, swallowing goat with a gulp.

"C'mon, Briggs, what are you waiting for? Join in!" I kept singing. Louder, louder, till I was near screaming. Blood vessels bulged in my neck. My temples pounded. *"Where are me boots, me noggy noggy boots, they've all gone for beer and tobacco! The leather's kicked about and the soles are all worn out, and my toes are looking out for better weather!"*

I could hear shouts of "Shut up!", sounds of men stirring, Dexter saying, "It's Nick! Down by the shore!"

Briggs still stared at me, his mouth hanging open, bits of meat stuck between his teeth.

I burst my lungs singing. *"I feel sick in the head and I haven't been to bed since first I came ashore with me plunder! I see centipedes and snakes and I'm full of pains and aches, and I think that I should push out over yonder!"*

By this time the entire camp had gathered, save Elizabeth.

I stopped singing, panting, my chest heaving. Dexter laid a gloved hand on my arm. "It's all right."

Sweet grabbed a meaty bone from Briggs. "Ye coward! What do ye mean by eating the goat all yourself?"

Briggs cast me a dark look. "My belly's about stuck to my backbone. I'm hungry all the time and it hurts. I got to have meat, I do. Red meat."

"Oh," said Dexter. "Like none of the rest of us have bellies or backbones."

Sweet sighed. "Well, boys, looks like grub's on. Garret, divide up the meat. Equal portions for everyone, including Elizabeth. None for Briggs. He's eaten his lot and more."

"Aye, sir," said Garret.

Back at the shelter, I woke Elizabeth. "Here, eat this."

"What is it?"

"Food."

She took it from me with trembling hands.

While she ate, I ate too, afterward licking my fingers over and over. When I was finished, I lay back down, crying softly. Because my heart ached for Ninny, and because I wanted more.

Two weeks before Christmas, Elizabeth sat up, her eyes clear of fever. The next day, she stepped out of the shelter for the first time in over three weeks. Like a child on Christmas morn, she gazed about her at all the new arrivals.

I told her how none of the others had survived, so far as we knew. Cole, Walker, Cook, Duff, and others, all gone. She just nodded, her jaw set in that now familiar line.

That evening, in celebration of Elizabeth's recovery, everyone gathered round a fire, where we sang sea chanteys, and everyone had a swallow of grog. My heart warmed from the grog and from seeing Elizabeth smile, throwing her head back to laugh. She sang softly, coughing sometimes, blushing at the bawdy words, whispering to me between songs that she'd grown up listening to those songs, and by fire, it was good to sing them finally!

Then Garret began to sing a ballad. His voice filled my insides like hot syrup in snow, the tenor tones rich and warm. Tears misted my eyes and I brushed my face with my glove. *"And it's home, dearie, home! oh, it's home I want to be. My topsails are hoisted, and I must out to sea, for the oak, and the ash, and the bonny birchen tree, they're all a-growin' green in the North Countree; oh, it's home, dearie, home! oh, it's home I want to be."*

I heard sighs all round. A sniffle or two. Elizabeth grasped my hand. Her eyes shimmered. "We'll get there someday," I whispered. "I promise."

She laid her head on my shoulder. Warm, delicious feelings flooded me, and I looked out across the group. Sweet, Garret, Dexter, all had that misty-eyed look too. But when I looked at Briggs, it was like an icicle stabbing my heart. He sat by himself, sucking the marrow out of one of Ninny's bones, staring at Elizabeth with hard, narrowed eyes. And in the depths of his eyes I saw a meanness and a hunger, the way he must have looked at Ninny before he slit her throat.

CHAPTER
18

J'd heard the yarn many a time—in the fo'c'sle, lounging round the windlass during the dogwatch. It was a true story about the whaleship *Essex* from Nantucket, about how she was stove by a maddened sperm whale and sank in the middle of nowhere, leaving behind twenty men in three whaleboats to survive best they could with just a few ships' biscuit between them. They did survive. A few of them, anyways. They survived by killing and eating their mates.

It was Briggs' favorite yarn.

Even now, when we huddled round the fire as lights danced and swirled above our heads in the cold, endless Arctic night, Briggs told it all the time, ignoring everyone who told him to shut up.

Whenever he told it, he giggled, a crazy, hungry laugh that made goose pimples crawl over my flesh as if it were my bones split in two, crunched between teeth; as if it were my marrow being sucked and swallowed.

Finally, sick of telling him to shut up, Sweet flung aside his pipe and lit into Briggs, giving him a black eye and a fat lip that stuck out so far that for three days Briggs had to pour water into his mouth from above if he wanted a drink. After that, Briggs didn't say anything. Just stared at Elizabeth. Licked his lips. Stared and stared.

It was Christmas. I lay awake, knowing it wasn't time to get up yet. Outside was still and terrible quiet, as if the Arctic held its breath. It had usually been at this time of morning that Ninny had bleated to be milked. I missed Ninny. I missed Aunt Agatha, too. I imagined her bustling down the stairs into the parlor to find Dexter and me under the Christmas tree, poking packages. I imagined her saying, "So I expect ye'll want to open them? Well, Dexter and Nicholas Robbins, not before ye've had your porridge and not before you're dressed and scrubbed." I felt the familiar press of hot tears that came whenever I thought of home. Would I ever see it again?

After setting more wood on the fire, I lay back down, already frozen to the bone. Beside me, Elizabeth stirred. "You awake?" I whispered, trying not to disturb Dexter and Garret.

"Aye."

"I have something for you."

"You do? For me?"

"I made it." From my pocket I pulled out a gift, wrapped in sailcloth and tied with hemp. "Merry Christmas."

She untied the bow and unwrapped the cloth, eyes gleaming in the firelight. "Why, it's a wood statue of my father."

"Aye. Standing and a-smoking his pipe. For you to remember him by."

"Thank you, Nicholas. I'll treasure it always."

A warm glow spread through my middles as she looked at me.

"I have something for you too," she said.

"For me?"

"Who else, silly?" She pulled out a pair of goatskin mittens from inside her fur parka. "Here. Merry Christmas, Nicholas Robbins."

I smiled. It was a good gift and a sad gift, all at the same time. "Thank you. I really need them." I tried them on, satisfied that they were a good fit.

So we lay there, each admiring our gifts, Elizabeth caressing the lines of the statue. The legs, the hat, the pipe . . . She sighed. "It's like I can smell the tobacco smoke right now."

I sniffed the air. Aye, it strangely reeked of tobacco smoke.

Then I heard a scrape of boot outside the shelter, a rummaging of something, and Henry Sweet's voice bellowing, "All hands! All hands on deck! We've got ourselves a situation!"

The hard bread was gone. Every last crumb. Gone.

"One of ye has stolen the biscuit!" Sweet marched up and down the line of us men. "If ye return it now, I'll pretend it never happened. But if we find it on ye, or if ye gets fat and blubbery while the rest of us poor folks starves thin as a rail, why, you'll wish ye never heard the name o' Henry Sweet, by fire, and that's the truth of it!"

Of course no one said anything, but we all stared at Briggs. Briggs gave us a dark look and curled his hand into a fist. "First man that accuses me gets it."

"Shut your trap, Briggs, I've had enough of ye," growled Sweet. "Search the camp, boys."

An hour later, after lighting every oil lamp, turning the camp upside down and inside out, and poking round for places the hard bread could have been buried, we gathered back round Sweet.

Nothing. No biscuit, nothing.

Sweet poked tobacco into his pipe and set it alight. The icicles hanging from his mustache and eyebrows glowed orange. "I don't know 'bout the rest of ye fellows, but I'm 'bout ready to eat me pipe. We've got to double our efforts for hunting. Get ready to go within the hour. And if I find anyone keeping what he caught to himself, he'll be what's in the stewpot. Now fetch me a whale, boys. Dismissed."

When I returned to the shelter, Elizabeth declared, "I'm going hunting with you."

My jaw flapped open. *A woman go hunting? Elizabeth? What does she know about hunting?* I shook my head. "I—I don't think that's a good—"

"You can either come with me or not, Nicholas Robbins, I don't care, but I'm not staying here acting like I don't have legs and arms and a brain like the rest of you. I'm going to fetch me some food, and that's that. Now are you coming or not?" She moved to the entrance, and I realized she was all ready to go, knapsack on her back, whale lance in her hand. Two blond braids dangled out from under her hood. Her jaw was set, and on her face was a look of the purest determination I'd ever seen.

I licked my lips, aware that both Garret and Dexter were listening beside me, saying nothing, just listening and probably waiting to hear what intelligent thing I'd say to her to make her change her mind.

"Uh—well," I stammered, my face hot as a boiling trypot. "Uh—well, all right, I guess."

"Then it's settled. Grab your things, Nicholas. I swear my teeth are going to fall out unless I get something to chew."

Elizabeth and I didn't do any better or worse at hunting than anyone else. Fact was, for the next two weeks, all we had to eat between eleven people was our usual whale oil and a young seal. And we didn't even kill it. It was dead already and partially eaten by a bear, likely. The bear had peeled the skin and blubber from the seal, leaving the red meat. We cooked it and stored it frozen. It made for a couple mouthfuls a day.

One day Elizabeth and I hacked down into a tundra pond, hoping to find fish. Took us two days, even with Dexter and Garret's help, and by the end of it, all we found in the bottom of the pond was more tundra. The pond was frozen solid. "Tundra, anyone?" Dexter had joked.

But no one laughed. Garret just tossed down his harpoon and stomped off.

Another day Elizabeth and I climbed over the jumble of ice ridges and prowled the sea ice, setting pieces of wood atop the ice as markers to guide us back to camp. Elizabeth, whose ears and eyes I learned were very keen, heard a breath behind her and then spotted a nose poking through the ice. "Seal," she whispered.

By the time we crept over, the seal was gone, the tiny hole only a circle of rippling slush. I stood poised over the hole, iron drawn back, waiting for it to breathe again. Five minutes . . . Ten . . . How long could a seal hold its breath? My muscles burned. My arm wobbled. Just as the iron began to drop, Elizabeth took the same position with her lance, her eye hungry as a hunter's, her jaw set. For many hours we took turns like that, waiting for the seal to breathe again. For the sound of exhaling. For a quiver in the iced-over slush. "It has to breathe again," I whispered.

"Of course it does, Nicholas." Elizabeth's voice sounded

drawn and thin. "But don't you think it has more than one breathing hole? Likely it's miles away by now."

It was a cold, long, seal-less, hungry, hungry day.

It came like a thief in the night. A fox. Fur white as winter, eyes aglow in the light of the fire, it stealthily snapped up an old hen bone lying outside the shelter entrance and slipped away before either Elizabeth or I could react.

"Hey!" I shouted. "He stole our bone!"

"Never mind about that! Grab your iron and let's go!" Elizabeth was already on her feet. "Hurry, before he disappears!"

Like tomcats after a mouse, we seized our weapons and dashed out of camp. At once, air stabbed my lungs like ice shards. A rainbow halo surrounded the Arctic moon. Stars gleamed, scattered like silver dust. The tundra was still, motionless, except for the fox that trotted fifty yards away, glancing back every few steps. Chest heaving, black spots dancing before my eyes, I determined to catch him. We ran and ran, seeming to grow no closer, my legs beginning to give way, when, suddenly, he vanished.

"Must be his den!" said Elizabeth, still running, gasping for breath.

We hurried to where we'd last seen the fox. Sure enough, a shadowy hole gaped in the snow like an open mouth.

"He's down there." Elizabeth peered into the burrow, breathing hard. "Hiding."

"Now what?"

She stood, holding her lance like a spear. "We dig."

Several hours later, we returned to camp. A group of men, including Dexter and Garret, sat round a fire, drinking whale oil and spinning yarns. At our approach, Dexter stopped midyarn and stared. They all did.

Without a word, Elizabeth and I strode into the circle, where she cast the fox onto the ground, its throat stained crimson. She then hunched down by the fire, yanked off her mittens, and rubbed her hands over the flame. I squatted beside her, doing the same, feeling the eyes of everyone on us. Finally, she looked up, seeming surprised, as if realizing for the first time that everyone was there and that they were all staring at her. "Well, fellows, what are you waiting for? Skin the fox and fix us a meal. I'm starved."

A week later, long after the fox was consumed, the marrow licked and sucked out of every bony crevice, a storm blasted in from the north. All hunting parties were halted. We huddled in our shelters, freezing, bunched together for warmth. The wind shrieked through the shelter, finding every opening. Hoarfrost covered everything that wasn't flapping in the wind. The four of us lay in a row like sausages in a skillet—a frosty skillet, that is—squeezed so tight we had to roll over together or not at all. Even so, cold seeped through my clothing, through every thread, chilling my bones. My ears ached. I shook with hunger. Beside me, Elizabeth clutched the carving of her father in her mittened hand, hugging it to her chest, a distant look in her eyes.

What if the storm continues for weeks? I wondered. *What, then? Will we all die in our shelters, starved and frozen stiff? Already Sweet and Garret have scurvy, their gums swollen and stinky. Sweet's leg is drawn up so bad only his toe touches the ground as he limps about.* Again, terror hunched in my chest like a ball of ice. Only now, I swear, sometimes I heard it laughing at me.

Aye.

Sometimes in the dead of night, when everyone was sleeping, I heard it howling with laughter. Like some ghost in the wind. Horrible and insane.

CHAPTER
19

"**F**inished, Elizabeth?" I clutched the blubber knife and ducked my head down into my shoulders. I blinked against the snow. Ice pelted my cheeks.

"Not yet." Elizabeth's voice came from behind me. Ever since the night of the polar bear attack, I always went with her whenever she had to, well . . . do her womanly business. I turned my back and waited until she finished. Tonight she was taking a long time.

"You still there?" I asked, speaking loudly to be heard over the wind's constant howl.

"Don't peek."

I heard her teeth chattering. "Don't let the bear eat you."

"Very funny."

149

"Holler if he drags you away."

"Ha ha."

I stomped my feet, which were already starting to turn numb. *By fire, it's freezing out here! What's taking her so long?* "Anything I can do to help?"

"Nicholas!"

"Sorry."

I ran in place, thanking God for the millionth time that I wasn't built like a woman.

"Nick—listen. Did you hear that?"

"Hear what?"

"Listen."

I stopped running and bent my ear to the wind. There, faint on the wind, like a mermaid singing below the sea, was laughter. Why, it was the same laughter I'd heard many a night! Horrible and insane. "You—you can hear that too?"

"I've heard it every night for a long time."

"I thought it was just me. What is it, do you suppose?"

I heard a rustle of clothing. "I—I don't know." Then Elizabeth was tugging my arm. "C'mon, Nick, let's go back. I don't like it out here."

I waited until Elizabeth was asleep.

Then, quiet as a whisper, I got up, took the lantern, and went outside as if it were my turn to do business.

But I had other plans.

The wind had picked up. It sliced through my clothes as though they were made of paper. I held up my lantern, smelling the whale oil, and peered out into the darkness. Beyond my bright circle of swirling snow, I could see nothing. It was hard snow, whipped up from the ground, never melting, dry and stinging like sand. I coughed. My breath gusted white.

After I stopped coughing, I stood and listened.

The flap of canvas.

The forever howl of wind.

Icy snow prickling my coat and the lantern glass.

The hiss of flame.

Then, laughter.

Chills crawled over my scalp and down my spine. *By the devil. Something's out there.*

I took a deep breath, cold searing my lungs. Grabbing a lifeline and holding my lantern high, I moved in the direction of the laughter.

Soon after Dexter and the others had arrived, Sweet had ordered a perimeter rope strung like a fence round us, fastened to timbers driven into the snow. Lifelines spread from our camp out to the perimeter like the spokes of a wheel. The enclosed area was huge, the lifelines twice the length of a ship's deck in any direction. It was so that on nights like this, we could find our way back. Now I gripped the lifeline and moved away from camp, praying I wouldn't lose my way. Or drop the rope.

What in tunket do you think you're doing? Are you crazy? Go back to the shelter before you freeze, before you're lost forever! But I could no more stop what I was doing than I could have stopped myself from visiting Elizabeth in the captain's quarters when she was sick. It was something I had to do. I was crazy that way, I guess.

Up ahead, I saw a light. A faint glow, a blur of swirling white. As I drew closer, something moved within the light. A human. I extinguished my lantern. If I could see him, he might see me. Darkness wrapped round me, thick and heavy. I wanted to cough but didn't dare. Again I crept toward the light, the lifeline sliding through my mittens.

Gradually, I saw within the light. A man crouched over Thorndike's grave, a lantern and harpoon by his side.

I moved round so I could see his face.

It was Briggs. Wild and crazy-eyed.

In front of him the body lay exposed, heaps of gravel and snow pushed to the side. Atop the body lay several biscuit, and as I watched, Briggs shoved a biscuit into his mouth. He chewed and laughed, chewed and laughed, afterward pulling from inside his clothes what looked to be a strip of meat. He shoved this into his mouth as well, grinning and smacking his lips, throwing his head back and laughing. . . .

Meat . . . *Where did Briggs get meat? He's thawing it next to his skin.* . . .

With a sickening roll of my stomach, I dropped to my knees, unable to stand a moment longer.

It was meat . . . *fresh from the grave.*

In that instant, something moved behind me.

I whirled, my heart in my throat.

Elizabeth stood looking past me, her gaze fixed on Briggs. Her eyes grew large until I could see the whites all round. Her mouth opened. Closed. Opened. Then a piercing scream burst from her, gushing like blood from a whale.

I shot to my feet and clamped my hand over her mouth.

Too late.

Briggs was already standing, his harpoon in his hand.

Elizabeth tore my hand away. "You murderer!" she shrieked. "You—you *cannibal!*" She lunged toward him, clawing the air, but I grabbed her and held her back.

"No, Elizabeth!"

Saying nothing, stealthy as a hunter, Briggs slipped out of the circle of light.

"Quiet!" I said in Elizabeth's ear. With a whimper, Elizabeth ceased struggling. Except for the howl of wind, the night was suddenly silent. The hairs on the back of my neck prickled. *Briggs is cutting off our retreat to camp! He's . . .*

I heard a movement.

"Elizabeth, run!"

"But I don't have the lifeline!"

"Neither do I. Run!"

"Where to?"

I began to run, yanking her alongside me. "Anywhere! He's after us!"

We fled into the darkness.

My spine tensed, bracing for the ice-cold point of a harpoon. Terror surged like vomit. I heard the pummel of our footsteps, the swish of our clothing, Elizabeth's breathing, panicked and racing. I tasted fear, cold and metallic. *Find the perimeter fence. Follow it to a lifeline and then back to camp. Hurry!*

Farther and farther. *God help us! Where is the fence? We should have reached it by now!* My legs began to wobble. My heart skittered like a rabbit's. The swirling snow dipped and rolled, and I knew my head was spinning. My knees buckled and I fell.

Elizabeth knelt beside me.

Once again the night was silent. My chest heaved.

Where's Briggs? Has he lost us? Are we safe?

Slowly, I rolled over and sat up.

Elizabeth whispered in my ear, "Stay quiet. He doesn't know where we are."

One minute . . . Two . . .

Nothing but the snow . . .

The wind . . .

Between gusts, I glimpsed the light, distant now. It was time to go. We struggled to our feet, holding hands. And without a word we crept back toward the light. I knew that with the perimeter fence likely blown down, it was the only way to find the camp again.

Then, without warning, like a giant ship appearing out of the dense fog, something moved in front of us, blocking the light.

Briggs!

"Run!" I screamed.

Too late.

I saw an arm reach back. A sudden thrust forward. A harpoon released.

"No!" I leapt in front of Elizabeth.

But not before she exploded backward into the darkness, 'pooned through like a beast.

o! No!

Someone was screaming, and I realized it was me. *He's killed Elizabeth! God help me, he's killed Elizabeth!* Like a blind man, I stumbled through the storm, searching for her. "Elizabeth!"

Over the shrieking wind, I heard laughter. "Oh, Bones! Oh, Bones, where are you? I have something for you as well."

No! No!

Snow and tears blinded me. Again I braced for the cold stab of metal in my back. A dagger. Another harpoon. "Elizabeth!" I cried, knowing she couldn't answer, knowing she was . . .

I stumbled over something and fell hard, scraping my cheek on the snow.

A body.

Elizabeth's.

I scrambled to her side.

At the same time, I heard claws scraping.

A huff of breath.

A roar.

A scream. A man's scream. "Blood and thunder, a bear! Get him off me! Get him—"

A strangled, gurgling cry.

Beside me, Elizabeth moved and groaned. *She's alive!*

I tried to pull her to her feet. "Run, Elizabeth! Hurry! A bear has Briggs!"

Horrified, I realized she couldn't move. The harpoon pinned her to the ice. I grabbed it and pulled with all my strength. Behind me, I heard a crunching. Like bones. My skin crawled. My hair stood on end.

Please, God!

Then Elizabeth was free from the ice, the harpoon still lodged in her shoulder. I heard her cry with pain. With a strength I didn't know I possessed, I tossed her over my shoulder, harpoon and all, and began to run.

I expected to feel claws in my back, teeth on my scalp, the full weight of a polar bear upon me, my bones snapping like twigs. I heard Elizabeth gasping. My own panicked breath. I ran until the sounds of the bear faded and I heard nothing but the wind. I ran forever, until we collapsed behind a snowdrift. Elizabeth sobbing. Tears freezing on my cheeks.

"I thought you were dead," I finally said.

Her teeth chattered. Her body shook. "We're lost, aren't we?"

I didn't answer. I held her close, wishing I could protect her, knowing I was helpless. The Arctic was too powerful. We were too small. Too human. Too alone.

"We're lost, aren't we?" she asked again.

"Aye. We're lost."

Endless darkness.

The wind, bone-numbing and relentless. Howling, howling.

My eyes watering.

Constant cold.

My feet, my hands, my face, blocks of ice.

It was a frozen hell. And us lost within it.

"Leave me," Elizabeth said when she could no longer walk. We huddled behind another snowdrift, trying to find relief from the wind. Already she'd walked with me for what seemed miles, both hands wrapped round the harpoon to keep it steady as I tried to support her. But finally, she'd collapsed. I'd carried her to the snowdrift. I could hardly see her. The milky white of the churning darkness surrounded us, blinding me. Her breath came in pants. "Leave me," she said again. "I'm going to die."

A heaviness filled my chest. "No. You're not going to die, Elizabeth."

"Listen to me. Save yourself. I—I want you to live."

I pressed my cheek to hers. Tasted the salt of her tears. "Aye, I want to live, but not without you. We belong together."

"You—you always had a hard head."

"No harder than yours." I pulled her close, wishing I could take her pain away, wishing for the thousandth time that it was me who was 'pooned instead of her. "I'll never leave you. I'll not let you die. Not while I have breath in my body."

"Nicholas?"

"Yes?"

Her mittened hand touched my cheek. "You're a good man. The kindest, nicest, dearest friend I've ever had. My—my only friend."

My throat clogged and I could say nothing. I held her for a long while, until the cold crept in like poison, numbing everything. Finally, I pushed myself to my feet. If we stayed longer, we'd freeze to death. "Elizabeth? Can you walk?"

There was no answer. My stomach crawled with fear. "Elizabeth?" I put my ear next to her mouth, almost crying with relief when I felt a puff of warm breath. Either she was asleep, or she'd fainted. Breath burning, I scooped her up and heaved her over my shoulder. It was no easy task with a harpoon in the way. My knees trembled, wanting to buckle, but I steeled my knees, set my jaw, and began to walk.

First one foot, then the other.

One foot, then the other . . .

One foot, then the other . . .

The cold numbed my thoughts, froze the song I was singing so that I sang the same words again and again. *Think, Nicholas! Think!* I imagined returning home. I imagined the warm smell of a fire in the stove. I imagined Aunt Agatha telling me to set the table for supper, the taste of hot biscuits, jam, baked beans, clam chowder. *I will return home. I will. Remember the cupola? One day, I'll gaze out of it again with my spyglass.* I tried to picture the cupola, but it kept slipping away, a frozen thought, lost in the churning wind. I wanted to cry but couldn't remember why I was sad, or where I was, or why I carried this heavy thing over my shoulder.

Suddenly, my knees buckled. The snow stung my chin, and my mouth snapped shut, ice in my teeth. A grunt of air spilled out of my lungs; snow clogged my ear. The heavy load on my shoulder mercifully fell off.

Darkness gathered, darker than the night. It seeped through my skin, pressed on my brain, clawed down my spine, and grasped my heart. . . .

I blinked—an icy, leaden blink, one eyelid frozen shut. *So cold . . . Just sleep. . . . Just sleep. . . .*

Then I saw something through the darkness. It was as if the night had parted and I could see forever, though the snow kept swirling and it was a long, long ways away. Shapes in the darkness. Different shapes. Different from snowdrifts, from the endless flat tundra. I smelled smoke. Saw dim squares of light.

I'm dreaming. It's a nice dream—heaven, maybe.

A spark of warmth fluttered inside me. Little at first, then swelling. And with the spark's swelling, I pushed the heavy darkness away with a will. *No! Elizabeth can't die! Not while I have breath in my body!*

Slowly, as though someone else were moving, not me, I grabbed a handful of snow and mashed it into my face.

Wake up! If you don't wake up now, you'll die!

I staggered to my feet, reeling like a drunkard, and began to drag Elizabeth toward the shapes. She was heavy. So heavy. My hands were blocks of wood, unable to grasp anything. One step. Another. Many steps. Miles, maybe.

Then the shapes came alive. Bursting out of the snow. Barking, growling. Warm breath, snapping teeth, and hot tongues surrounded us. I heard shouts. Voices. Men, women. Many people. Emerging from the ground. I felt hands on me, a tickle of fur.

"Help," I blurted, before I collapsed alongside Elizabeth in a drift of snow.

Warmth.

A sod home.

Walls of whale ribs and driftwood. Gigantic jawbones supporting a sod roof. A skylight covered with dried intestine. The stink of grease and oil and urine. Children stared, giggling, clutching dolls of ivory dressed in bird skins. Men, lips pierced with bone, studied us, talking among themselves. Women smiled, their teeth blackened and worn, chins tattooed. They pried open my mouth and put food on my tongue. I swallowed, moaning.

I heard a scream, Elizabeth's, and knew they'd pulled the harpoon from her shoulder. Voices murmured.

Many hands rubbed my bare skin. Feeling—hot and needle-like—returned. *It hurts!* Someone was thrashing, crying out, "Elizabeth!"

"I'm here, Nicholas, I'm all right."

So tired . . .

I lay between two caribou skins, fur soft against my flesh.

When I opened my eyes, three children sat cross-legged, staring at me. They looked at one another and giggled. And at the sound of a man's voice, the children scooted off the platform where I lay and ran across the floor of driftwood and baleen, squatting against the far wall, still watching me, still giggling.

The house was crammed with people, twelve, fifteen of them, squatting, standing, staring. About fifteen feet by ten, the house appeared to be half underground, domed at the top. It was surprisingly warm, though the only sources of heat were two seal-oil lamps and the wind still raged outside. When the people saw me looking round, they smiled, speaking words that sounded like water gurgling over a creek bed.

Elizabeth slept behind me on the platform, cocooned within her own deerskin blankets, her wounded shoulder bound with more skins. The look on her face was relaxed and peaceful, her breathing steady.

I smelled meat cooking. Hunched over one of the lamps, a woman stirred something in a stone pot set upon a frame of antlers. Like the others, her cheekbones were broad, her skin bronzed, her eyes and hair black as a raven's. Another woman handed me a pot of liquid. I was thirsty and started to drink it but stopped when they all laughed—warm laughter like butter.

Eyes twinkling in the dim light, the woman shook her head. And she made the motion of washing her face. I dipped into the bowl and washed my face. Smelled horrible, it did. Like . . . like pee! Grimacing, I hastily scrubbed my face.

Just then, Elizabeth stirred. "Nick? Where are you?"

I set down the bowl. "You all right?"

She crinkled her nose. "Blood and thunder, what's that smell?"

"Nothing . . . I—"

"You look different."

"Me?"

"You look . . . cleaner. I—I can see your skin."

I touched my cheeks. Why, the pee had cut through my layers of grime, filth, and grease! My skin was right clean! Pee-clean. "Ancient recipe for soap, I guess. You sure you're all right?"

"My shoulder's stiff and aches something terrible." Elizabeth smiled, though her eyes spoke of her pain. "Don't think I want to be heaving people over my shoulder for a while, or wandering lost in a blizzard."

"Are you sure you're all right?"

She sighed, and I knew she was remembering the grave, remembering what she'd seen. "I guess. Not exactly something I wanted to see."

"I'm sorry. Sorry it happened."

"Me too. But it's done now, and I'm tired of wasting my time pining over things that are done and gone."

Meanwhile, Woman Who Cooks, as I'd begun to think of her, dished out steaming pieces of boiled meat from the pot and set them on a plate of baleen, while another woman handed us each a piece of dried whale blubber and motioned for us to eat. *"Maktak."*

Elizabeth and I chewed the blubber, aware that everyone watched. Oil seeped down my chin.

Several of the women approached and touched Elizabeth's corn-silk braids, caressed her blond head. There was a murmur of excitement. More natives came to touch Elizabeth's hair. One woman pointed at Elizabeth's eyes, then mine.

Woman Who Cooks then selected a piece of meat from the baleen plate—the flipper of a seal—and handed it to me, along with an ivory knife. She did the same for Elizabeth. People seemed pleased as we began to chew on the flippers. Then, one by one, they each chose a piece of meat from the plate and began to eat.

I could hardly eat fast enough to keep up with the raging hunger in my stomach. The meat was tender, dark, with a pleasant taste.

"They've given us the best pieces," Elizabeth said, studying them as they studied her, grease glistening on her cheeks. "They're treating us like we're their honored guests."

"I don't suppose they've seen people like us before."

When we finished eating, licking our fingers of every tidbit, the men began talking to me, motioning with their hands. It seemed as if they were asking questions, as if they wanted answers. Meanwhile, natives entered the house through a hole in the floor, talked, stared, smiled, caressed Elizabeth's hair, and then left, only to be replaced by others—sometimes whole families, by the look of it. It seemed we were the village attraction.

"We're from the whaleship *Sea Hawk*," I said, talking to the man who appeared to be the leader. He was older than the rest, but not as old as the gray-haired man who sat in the corner, gumming blubber with his toothless mouth. "We were wrecked and our ship sank."

A look of confusion spread over the chief's face. He turned to the other men and they hunched down, talking with one another.

"We need help," Elizabeth added. "Our friends are still out there. They don't have any food." She made the motion of eating, shaking her head when they offered her more meat. "No, we must go and find them. Bring them here."

Still the confusion.

"It's no use," I said. "They don't understand."

Elizabeth pointed to my ivory knife. "Carve a picture for them. Everyone understands pictures."

Of course! I reached for my clothes to get dressed, but the women immediately waved me away and handed me a set of skins. Soft and warm they were, sewn with threads of sinew. The women smiled as I pulled them on. I thanked them, hoping they understood how grateful I was. Dressed now in my furs, I stood to my full height. Natives gasped, mouths open in astonishment, gazing up at me from no higher than my chest. Again, they spoke to one another rapidly, their voices excited.

Soon I was carving pictures into walls of driftwood. People crowded round me, pointing, talking. The whaleship, the shipwreck, four people in a whaleboat, our camp at shore . . .

CHAPTER 21

*T*he dogs ran. I heard the huff of their breath, saw the white steam, the tongues flapping. Paws pummeled the snow. Legs pumped in long, easy strides. The baleen sled runners glided beneath us, snow crunching. Jeweled stars blanketed the sky.

Elizabeth followed on a second sled, behind which followed a third sled. Surrounded by furs and the frigid air of endless night, we would soon arrive at camp.

Soon . . . soon . . .

After I had carved pictures into driftwood, they had loaded each of us onto a sled, bundled in furs. At a command the dogs immediately ceased their yipping and whining, dug in, and bounded away.

Soon . . . soon . . .

"The sea! There's the sea!" cried Elizabeth.

I saw the vague outline of dunes, of pressure ridges beyond. The natives *had* understood me! We were searching for the camp!

At a single command from the native who steered the sled, the dogs changed direction and headed northeast. We had been traveling along the shore for perhaps only a quarter of an hour when suddenly the dogs' ears pricked up and they began to whine, running faster. I glimpsed a glow of orange in the distance.

"Fire! We've found them!" I laughed, joy bubbling like a happy melody.

Dexter, Garret, Sweet, and the others crept out from their shelters, faces smeared with grime, eyes shrunken, staring slack-jawed as the sleds came to a halt and the dogs lay down in their harnesses, panting, taking bites of snow.

Thin as a bone, Dexter shuffled toward us. "We thought you were dead. We found human remains. Signs of a polar bear attack. We thought that—we thought—"

I'd never seen Dexter weep before.

He flung his arms round me and sobbed. I held my big brother, tears lodged in a lump in my throat. Then someone else was there. Elizabeth. Wrapping her good arm round us. Then others—Garret, Sweet—limped over, until we formed a circle of arms and bodies.

Suddenly, Garret whooped a big holler that got the dogs to howling. "We're saved!" he screamed, head back to the heavens. "Thank God, we're saved!" He began to dance a little jig, but had to stop when he erupted in a fit of coughing. Bent over, he spit out a tooth, blood spattering the snow. "Didn't need it anyways," he said with a scurvy smile.

I introduced my friends to the natives. "They saved our lives,"

I told them. The natives didn't seem to know what to do with an outstretched hand, but my friends grabbed their hands anyway and pumped them, grinning like Cheshire cats.

The native men caught a seal that day, and we had a feast before we broke camp. We sat round a fire, hands glistening with grease, cheeks and bellies distended with meat, as I told the story of what had happened that night, the night Elizabeth was 'pooned, the night Briggs was killed by a polar bear.

"I ain't never heard of such a thing," Garret said after I finished.

Dexter squinted, waving smoke away. "We knew something bad had happened, what with the biscuit we found at the grave and everything all—you know—messed up."

"But don't worry yourself none, Miss Elizabeth," said Garret. "We fixed up your papa's grave. Good as pie."

"'Tis a mercy ye weren't killed," said Sweet. "That Briggs was a bad apple, he was. Rotten to the core."

Elizabeth raised her cup for a toast, eyes shining, suddenly looking much older than her sixteen years. "Here's to better days. Days of good health, new friendships, and someday, home, wherever that might be."

We all raised our cups. "Hear! Hear!"

As we broke camp, Garret sang a chantey, "Jolly Rovin' Tar," and everyone joined him, splitting the Arctic night with our lungs. And as we gathered our things together, we gave the natives all the tools, rope, whale oil, sailcloth, coal, and whatever else they wanted. It was theirs in return for our lives. All of us agreed. The owners of the *Merimont* need never know.

We spent the rest of winter and all of spring with the natives. Briggs had been wrong about them. Wrong when he said they were stupid, savage beasts. Of course, I don't know why I was so surprised—Briggs was wrong about lots of things.

They divided the ten of us up, two into each of their sod homes. They welcomed us like long-lost brothers, or a long-lost sister, as the case may be. They taught us to hunt seals through breathing holes in the ice, took us south along the river to hunt caribou with sinew-backed bows and arrows tipped with antler, taught us to make bolas of sinew and ivory, which we flung into flocks of seabirds. The women sewed each of us an outfit of fur clothing, first softening the skins by chewing them.

Evenings we all sat round the communal gathering house with our new friends, tried our hand at wrestling, weight lifting, and other feats of strength, afterward dancing to chants and drums, or listening to them tell yarns. And though we couldn't understand them, just watching their hand motions and expressions and laughter, their stories seemed like magic, as though we were in another world and another time—which we were, I expect.

Come March, as openings began to appear in the ice, the whales returned. The natives set up temporary camps on the ice, and if a whale was spotted, it was a mad dash, sometimes on foot, sometimes in their umiaks—boats of driftwood and sealskin—to harpoon the whale. A successful kill made for long days of butchering and celebration. The meat was carried back to the village, where it was stored in ice cellars in the permafrost. Unlike us Yankees, the natives used the entire carcass, down to the bones. It was either eaten or put to practical use.

The snow started melting in May, exposing bare patches of earth. The air smelled of moss, of dampness, of spring. Our camp lay next to a frozen river, and the ice atop the river melted and gurgled down to the sea. We exchanged our winter clothing for summer furs, which all of us had helped sew despite the gestured protestations of the native men that sewing was women's work. Meanwhile, as the ground thawed into a spongy soup of moss and lichen, we moved from our underground homes into tents of caribou hide and sealskin. Then, in the middle of June, on a day when the sun never set, the ice block at the river's mouth suddenly released and water gushed out over the sea ice.

Finally, in July of 1853, the ice unlocked and the summer sea opened. It was time to leave. We packed our belongings into our whaleboats and gathered on the shore to bid good-bye to our hosts. To Nogasak, whom I'd first called Woman Who Cooks. To her husband, Kunasluk, the chief. To their little daughter, Pannigabluk, who taught us to play kickball and a game with fat white hen bones. To others whose names and faces will remain with me forever. After giving them gifts—scrimshaw, new dolls, a bone flute—we shoved off and set sail, waving until those on shore disappeared into the fullness of the Arctic summer.

Several weeks later, not far off the coast, as seabirds screeched and circled the nearby bluffs, we spied upward of thirty sails in the distance. Soon a whaleship approached under shortened sail. I heard the snap of canvas, the groan of hemp, the shouted commands. Saw the stares of the people aboard as they hove to. A girl's voice asked, "Mother, who are they? Have they come to trade?"

"Ahoy there!" cried a man. He leaned over the rail, watching as our whaleboats touched the hull. "Who are ye and what be the manner of your business?"

"Captain Coggeshall," said Garret, standing up as he pulled down his fur hood. Red hair caught the sunlight.

The captain blinked. "Why, if I didn't know better, I'd say 'twas Garret . . . Garret . . ."

"Hix, sir."

"Yes, Garret Hix. I thought ye had signed aboard the *Sea Hawk.*"

"I did, but we was shipwrecked up north last fall. We spent the winter with the natives."

"Shipwrecked! So *that's* what happened! When the *Sea Hawk* didn't return, everyone feared the worst. Where's Ebenezer Thorndike? Where's the *Merimont*? Last anyone knew, she sailed in your company."

Garret glanced at us and sighed. "They're gone, Captain. We're all that's left. Ten of us from the *Sea Hawk,* including Thorndike's daughter, Elizabeth."

The captain's wife had come to stand beside him. At Garret's words, she paled, but seemed to recover quickly. "Well, Obed, where's your manners? Don't just leave them yammering from below, invite everyone aboard. Certain Miss Elizabeth would enjoy a bath and some real clothes. I've dresses that will fit her fine. I'll tell Cook to prepare hot coffee and a hot meal for everyone."

Soon we were all aboard the *Alabaster,* Garret's old whaling ship. The captain and mates wanted to hear everything—where we'd traveled, how many whales we'd taken, how the shipwreck had come about, how we had survived. True to her word, Mrs. Coggeshall whisked Elizabeth off. In a couple of hours, she emerged from the companionway to where we yakked round the wheel, her hair neatly washed and curled, her skin scrubbed yet sun-browned against a gown of pale yellow, Mrs. Coggeshall beaming from behind her. We men were quiet for a spell, as if Elizabeth were suddenly a stranger.

As for me, my heart twirled. "You're looking fine today, Miss Elizabeth."

All the men added their agreement. "Right fine." "Darn pretty." "You clean up nice." "Your parents would be proud."

Elizabeth smiled sweetly, as if she'd never been harpooned, never driven a dog team, never devoured raw meat, never skinned a caribou. "Why, thank you, everyone." She turned to the captain, who seemed just as smitten as the rest of us. "It's a right fine day, Captain Coggeshall. A right fine day. Don't you think?"

"Aye, Miss Thorndike. A fine day."

"So," she said, peering off into the distance, "when can we go home?"

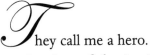

*T*hey call me a hero.

Survivor of the Arctic. Rescuer of Miss Elizabeth Thorndike, who was 'pooned by a madman.

But I like to think the natives were the heroes. For they saved Elizabeth and me when it was certain we would have died. I don't know if heroes have strokes of luck; I expect it's all part of the package. Some bravery, some luck. But somehow, deep down, I really don't believe it was luck at all. I was led to the village. Call it God, call it the will to survive; it doesn't matter. All I know is that on such a dark night in a snow-storm, I shouldn't have been able to see the village even if I had been standing in its cen-ter. But see it I did, from far, far, away.

The news of what had happened

traveled quickly through the fleet. A flood of gifts arrived—food and clothing. The captains of the other whalers offered us jobs. Captain Coggeshall told us the *Alabaster*'s hold was near full and she was headed home to New Bedford soon as she caught a couple more whales. He said he'd be happy to take anyone along who wanted to go. Anxious to make up for their losses aboard the *Sea Hawk*, though, most of my shipmates signed aboard other whalers, Dexter and Garret among them. Whaling was good this season, the best, or so everyone said. As Garret and Dexter left to board the *Vagabond*, Garret shook my hand. "I owe you my life, Bones. We all do. Write to me, will you?"

I nodded, squeezing his hand tight, unable to speak.

Dexter clapped me on the back, and then gave me a hug. "You're a good man, Nick," he said, his voice thick. "The best there is."

"Aye."

"You'll be a great carver. You already are. Father would be proud."

"Aye."

"Take care, brother."

"You too."

"I'll be home someday. I'll come visit your shop."

"Aye, Dex. I know."

'Twas a considerable grand mansion. Just as I remembered it.

I rapped softly and, without waiting for an answer, opened the front door and stepped inside. "Aunt Agatha?"

Then she was there, reaching up to wrap her floury arms round my neck. "Bless me, why, bless me, if it isn't little Nicholas!" After hugging me a minute or so, she pulled back, wiping her eyes on her apron. "They said ye weren't dead after all. They said ye was even a hero. My stars and body, to think of it! My Nicholas, a hero!"

I couldn't say anything. My throat tightened, my grin so wide I thought I'd split my ears. *By fire, it's good to be home!*

Aunt Agatha straightened herself. "Have ye forgotten your manners, young Nicholas? Introduce me to your friend."

I motioned for Elizabeth to join me in the foyer. "Aunt Agatha, I'd like you to meet Miss Elizabeth Thorndike. She needs a home. I wrote and asked if she could stay here."

"So ye did."

"Can she?"

"Come here, girl, let me have a look at ye." Frowning, Aunt Agatha pulled Elizabeth toward her and studied her close. "Humph. Well, I'd say ye need some meat on them bones. I've got fresh biscuits coming out of the oven, and I'll put water on for tea. I've got some strawberry preserves folks declare be the best in New Bedford. What do ye say?"

Elizabeth smiled, casting a glance and a wink at me. "Aye. Biscuits, preserves, and tea sound wonderful, Miss Agatha."

"Well, don't stand a-gawking, young Nicholas, set the table."

"Aye, Aunt Agatha. Aye."

'Twas in the early morning, standing in the cupola as the sun painted the sky with purples and oranges, that I kissed Miss Elizabeth Thorndike right proper. Hair like corn silk, eyes blue as cornflowers, her lips were soft and warm, and she smelled of lilacs.

Afterward, we gazed out the cupola, a carved tooth, a cat of ivory, and a wooden statue of a man sitting beside us on the windowsill. Past New Bedford to the river we gazed, taking turns with the spyglass. Ships jammed the wharves. Several were out on the river, sails gleaming white, men clambering up the shrouds. I imagined the shouted commands, the greenies feeling awkward in their stiff new dungarees. "What do you see?" I asked, hugging her tight.

She smiled, handing me the spyglass. "Why, I see home, Nicholas Robbins. Take a look for yourself."

At one time, strolling through the streets of New Bedford, over the cobblestones and under the elms, past the apothecary, the livery, the blacksmith, you would have seen a sign hanging over the door of a shop, reading,

Nicholas Robbins
Extraordinary Carver
Est. 1854

And, if you peeked through the window, you would see Mr. Robbins at work, a tall, lean man, producing masterpieces so fine you would have gladly spent every penny in your pocket to own one. And if you went inside to the jangle of bells, you would have met Mrs. Robbins, a lovely woman with hair like corn silk, who would have taken your order with a smile and arranged for delivery. And, if you were especially lucky, you might happen to be there as three young girls marched in from school, hair like their mother's, two with eyes blue as cornflowers and one with eyes green as shamrocks. You would have seen the carver stop what he was doing and swing each child atop his shoulders, laughing as their hair dusted the rafters.

AUTHOR'S
NOTE

Since time immemorial whalers combed the warm waters of the world, taking whale after whale with little thought for the future, never dreaming that the plentiful "fish," as they called them, would one day hover on the brink of extinction. Through the centuries, the demand for whale products increased, reaching a peak in the mid-1800s. Whale oil was used as a lubricant and illuminant, as well as in soap making. Spermaceti, the waxy substance found only in the heads of sperm whales, was unsurpassed as a clear-burning oil. At that time, American whalemen obtained baleen from a species of whale called the right whale (so called because it was the "right" whale to hunt). Baleen was hard yet somewhat flexible and was used in many of the ways we use plastic today. In the mid-1800s, the hoopskirt was all the rage, and the demand for baleen skyrocketed, as baleen was necessary to maintain the skirt's fashionable shape.[i] But by this time, whales were becoming more and more difficult to find.

In July 1848, the bark *Superior* sailed north into the Bering Strait and discovered waters teeming with bowhead whales, a species previously unexploited by Yankee whalemen. Not only was the bowhead baleen far longer than the baleen of the right whale, but the bowhead were slow-moving, placid creatures that were blanketed in fat, yielding more than two and a half times the oil of a like-sized sperm whale.[ii] Word spread like floodwater, and soon the western Arctic was filled with whalers jostling for position. Over the next several decades, Yankee whalers proceeded to harvest an Arctic whale population that had sustained the native peoples for millennia. As the bowhead population began to decline, whalers pushed farther and farther north, sometimes spending winters encased in ice. Two whaling disasters occurred in 1871 and 1876, in which a total of forty-five whalers were crushed in ice—the ships, whale oil, equipment, and fifty men, lost.[iii]

Life aboard a whaler in the eighteenth and nineteenth centuries was anything but grand. A whaler was really a floating factory. Its purpose was to hunt whales and process them while at sea. The men worked long hours—four hours on, four hours off, day in and day out—unless there was a storm, a whale chase, or a whale to render. In that case, they labored until the work was done. The job was dangerous, too. The leading causes of death were disease, falls from aloft, and encounters with whales. Adolescent male sperm whales were especially dangerous. A sperm whale could use its flukes to great effect, often smashing boats to splinters and sending men to the deep. As Nick realized in his first hunt, a hundred things can and did go wrong in a whale chase. And once the whale was brought alongside, the danger was far from over. Sharp spades and cutting knives sliced off many a foot or finger, and the blubber swinging inboard weighed tons.

The captain of a whaler bore a heavy responsibility. It was his job not only to navigate dangerous, sometimes uncharted waters but also to train a crew of mostly inexperienced men to hunt and kill whales, to render the maximum amount of oil, and to deliver the payload home safely.[iv] If he failed, it was possible he would never command a whaler again. More often than not, the captain of a whaler was a competent mariner, fair-minded and decent. But the ship was an island of its own, and the captain its un-disputed master. In those days, it was believed that the crew was obedient only through the threat of punishment. Shipping laws allowed captains to maintain discipline through corporal punish-ment. It was not unusual for whaling captains to lock men in irons, carry a gun, lay on the lash, or hang sailors from the yardarms in an effort to maintain order, prevent desertion, and "motivate" the crew. These expectations were explicitly stated by Captain Mellen in 1857 on the whaler *Junior* after leaving New Bedford for a whaling voyage: "I mean to have order and fair dealing all around. And if anyone fails to do his duty the shipping laws of the United States give me authority to punish you exactly as I see fit—from irons in the brig to lashing or hanging at a yardarm."[v] What might be considered a more typical captain's speech occurred aboard the *America* in 1862: "Well, men, the land is behind us and I suppose you all know you are a-whaling. It is my duty to bring the vessel and every one of you back to port four years from now and with as much oil as we can get by rea-sonable attention to business. Now listen to me. When you are called, do your duty. If you are mean or ugly or fail to do your part or show any disrespect to your officers, you will be severely punished. We shall have no rebellion aboard this ship."[vi]

Nantucket, a small island town off the coast of Massa-chusetts, became the first whaling capital of the world. In the 1600s, whales were so plentiful that one could literally stand on the shores of Nantucket and see whales frolicking in the ocean. Nantucketers began their whaling careers by rendering beached whales. Soon they ventured out onto the open waters, and by the time of the Revolutionary War, Nantucketers roamed the

Atlantic, hunting sperm whales. The majority of the town's industry was devoted to whaling—cooperages, carpenter shops, sailmaking lofts, candleworks, and shipyards. Many of the town's leading men were either shipowners or worked as captains or mates aboard the fleet of whalers. As soon as they grew old enough, sons followed their fathers into the whaling life and worked their way up the ranks. But the face of whaling changed as the Pacific fishery opened, and whale crews were now gone for years rather than months. Whaleships necessarily became bigger, with a deeper draft to handle the demands of two-, three-, or four-year voyages. The Nantucket harbor was too shallow for these larger ships, and there were other coastal towns vying for a piece of the whaling pie.[vii] In the 1820s, New Bedford, Massachusetts, emerged as the new whaling capital. Like Nantucket, most of New Bedford was devoted to the whaling life. Children like Nick and Dexter, born into that environment, grew up with the scent of whale oil in their nostrils and dreams of the adventurous life.

But the realities of whaling soon took their toll. Fathers were separated from families for years on end, only to have to leave on another voyage soon after arriving home. Wives solved this problem to some extent by deciding to come along and raise their families aboard the ship, but this was a later development. The community suffered when too many men were lost at sea, killed or maimed. Sometimes the entire ship was lost, or it returned to port with inferior oil or with its holds empty, as whales became more and more scarce.

The captain and crew were paid according to how much whale oil they brought home. No oil, no pay. One-third of the oil's gross profits went to the owners. One-third went to supplies and maintenance of equipment. The final third was divided between captain and crew. The captain, the officers, the harponeers, and the cooper generally earned between 1/8 and 1/100, depending on their rank and experience. The experienced whalemen, the cook, and the steward took between 1/100 and 1/150 shares. The "greenies," or landlubbers, like Nick, earned from 1/150 to 1/200. A whaleman's share was called a "lay," so Nick would have signed on for a "1/200 lay." There are recorded instances in which a greenie ended up *owing* the owners money after the completion of the voyage. Owners charged the crew for insurance, for goods from the slop chest, and so on. A greenie like Nick would make purchases against his pay, and if the amount of oil taken was poor, he was in debt upon arrival in port! Sometimes, due to desertion and death, only a few of the original men returned to port to collect their wages. The average pay for a foremast hand at the end of a whaling voyage was less than twenty cents per day, one-third to one-half the amount he could have earned on land.[viii]

For the many men who found life aboard a whaler intolerable, desertion was an option frequently exercised. Indeed, so many men deserted in Hawaii that the port cities quickly developed strict rules to ensure that every sailor who came ashore returned that evening to his own ship. Hawaii had recently been proselytized by Christian missionaries, so the influence of scores of sailors on the lam and without much money in their pockets was considered less than desirable. Nick and Dexter experienced a Honolulu "welcoming committee" similar to that which must have greeted countless unlucky whalemen seeking to escape a life that hadn't lived up to their expectations.

After about 1860, it became increasingly difficult to obtain a crew for the less-than-glamorous occupation. New Bedford and Nantucket men were now likely to be the captains, the mates, the owners—the big money behind the ships—while the common crew was filled with whatever men they could find. Because of the extremes of the whaling life, the average age of the common whaleman was little more than twenty. Few sailors before the mast were over thirty years of age. Owners became so anxious to fill the ranks of their crew, they signed on anyone with warm blood, whether he had sailing experience, whether he could speak English, or whether he was a drunkard or even a convict. Whale crews became much like a floating League of Nations, a conglomeration of men from all parts of the world.[ix]

A word on language: the communities of both Nantucket and New Bedford were traditionally Quaker, developing language patterns modeled after the King James version of the Bible, liberally sprinkled with *thee*'s and *thou*'s and *ye*'s. By the mid-1800s, influences from other communities—and really, from other nations—began to be apparent, especially among the speech patterns of the younger generation. No longer wanting to be "old-fashioned," they gradually adopted the more common *you*. There was certainly a generation gap in the language patterns, which is reflected in *Voyage of Ice*. Even so, usage of *ye* versus *you* among individual speakers of that era was often arbitrary, as there were likely as many variations in speech as there were people.

After the rise and fall of the western Arctic whale fishery in the decades following 1850, the whaling industry continued to wane as alternative illuminants such as kerosene replaced the demand for whale oil. Fashions also changed, and by the early 1900s, other products replaced baleen.[x] For all intents and purposes, the glory days of the whaling era were at an end.

In 1946, alarmed by the decimation of the world whale populations, the International Whaling Commission (IWC) was established to maintain healthy whale populations and to regulate the whaling industry. At various times between 1946 and 1985, the IWC designated certain whale species as protected, established whale sanctuaries, and set limits on the number and type of whales that could be taken. Despite these efforts, whale populations continued to decline, and some species faced extinction. In 1985, the IWC issued a moratorium on commercial whale hunting, which remains in effect today. The IWC also regulates the hunting of whales for subsistence by native populations, striving to maintain a balance between continued growth of whale species and the honoring of cultural tradition.[xi]

It is this author's dream that all commercial whaling will cease forever and that all nations will recognize the value of a whale beyond its ability to provide humankind with products, but rather as a creature with its own fundamental right to existence, irrespective of humanity. It is this author's dream that our grandchildren and great-grandchildren can one day stand on the many shores of our planet and once again see whales frolicking in the ocean waters.

i. John R. Bockstoce, *Whales, Ice, and Men: The History of Whaling in the Western Arctic* (Seattle: University of Washington Press, 1986), 29, 165–166.

ii. Ibid., 91.

iii. Murray Lundberg, "Thar She Blows! Whaling in Alaska and the Yukon," ExploreNorth, http://www.explorenorth.com/library/yafeatures/bl-whaling.htm.

iv. Nathaniel Philbrick, *In the Heart of the Sea: The Tragedy of the Whaleship* Essex (New York: Viking, 2000), 200.

v. Chester S. Howland, *Thar She Blows! Thundering Adventures of Whaling and Mutiny* (New York: Wilfred Funk, 1951), 95–96.

vi. Ibid., 227.

vii. Albert Cook Church, *Whale Ships and Whaling* (New York: W. W. Norton, 1938), 17–18.

viii. Bockstoce, *Whales, Ice, and Men,* 35–37.

ix. New Bedford Whaling Museum, http://www.whalingmuseum.org.

x. U.S. Environmental Protection Agency, "Imprint of the Past: The Ecological History of New Bedford Harbor," http://www.epa.gov/nbh/html/whaling.html.

xi. International Whaling Commission, http://www.iwcoffice.org/iwc.htm.

GLOSSARY
of
SEA TERMS

aback – with the wind on the forward side of the sails, causing sails to be driven backward against the mast. Can happen accidentally or can be executed on purpose to stop a vessel's forward momentum.

abaft – toward the stern of a vessel; to the rear of. The word "abaft" is used in relation to an object—for example, "abaft the mainmast" or "abaft the beam."

aft – toward the stern of a vessel. The opposite of "ahead."

aloft – above the deck of the ship.

amidship shelter – an unenclosed flat-roofed shelter that provides a somewhat dry workspace. Spare whaleboats are stored on top.

amidships – in the center of the ship.

avast – to stop. "Avast hauling!" means "to stop hauling."

bark – a bark is usually a three-masted sailing vessel, with the fore- and mainmasts square-rigged and the mizzen fore-and-aft rigged.

beat – to make way to windward by zigzagging through a series of tacks.

binnacle – the housing of a ship's compass and lamp.

block – a rounded wooden case housing a pulley, used for lowering and lifting heavy loads. A line through a block forms a tackle.

bo'sun's chair – a flat seat

attached to ropes, used to hoist sailors aloft to repair rigging. (Bo'sun is short for *boatswain* and is pronounced BO-sun. The bo'sun was responsible for maintaining the rigging, sails, and hull.)

bow – the front of the ship (rhymes with "cow").

bowline – a sailor's knot used to form a loop in a line (pronounced BO-lin).

box the compass – to recite the thirty-two compass points in order and to understand their meaning.

brogan – a heavy leather shoe.

bulkhead – an interior partition or wall in a vessel.

bulwarks – the built-up side walls above the deck of a ship.

capsize – to overturn.

chantey – a song sung by sailors while at work. There are different chanteys for different types of work.

chocks – grooves in the forwardmost part of a whaleboat's bow through which the whaleline runs.

companionway – a stairway or ladder leading from one deck to another. On the main deck, the entrances to the companionways are sheltered in small raised housings, complete with doors to keep out the elements.

cooper – one who makes or repairs wooden tubs. The cooper was a vital part of a whaling crew, as he was responsible for making airtight casks that would hold up under extreme conditions.

courses – the large square sails that hang on a ship's lower yards.

crow's nest – a canvas shelter at the topgallant masthead. Used during the Arctic whale fishery, it protected sailors from the shoulders down from the wind.

cuddy – a small room or cupboard in a boat.

cupola – a raised observation room built on top of a roof, usually circular.

dipper – a metal bucket used to remove the oil from the trypots and pour it into the adjacent cooling tank.

dogwatch – the divided watch between four and eight in the evening, the first dogwatch being from four to six, the second from six to eight. Except for the helmsman and lookout, the men from both watches are allowed to relax during the second dogwatch.

doughboy – a heavy boiled dumpling often made with the meat of blackfish or porpoise.

duff – a boiled or steamed dumpling made with flour, lard, sugar, and dried fruit.

fall – the loose end of a rope and tackle.

fluke – one of the broad winged portions of a whale's tail.

fo'c'sle – the forward cabin of a ship, directly behind the bow and in front of the foremast. The crew's sleeping quarters are in the fo'c'sle. (Fo'c'sle is short for *forecastle* and is pronounced FOKE-sul.)

fore and aft – in a line parallel to the length of the ship.

foremast – the mast closest to the bow.

forward – toward the bow of the ship.

furl – to roll a sail to a yard.

gally – to frighten.

gangway – an opening at a ship's side where people embark and disembark. In a whaler, the cutting stage was erected off the gangway.

greenie – someone who has never shipped before and has yet to learn his duties. Also called a landlubber.

grog – an alcoholic beverage, especially diluted hot rum mixed with lemon juice and sugar.

grommet – a ring used to fasten a sail to its stay (the line used to support the mast).

gunwale – the upper edge of the ship's side (pronounced GUN-ul).

harponeer – the crewman who tosses, casts, darts, or pitches the harpoon. (One never *throws* a harpoon.) Only landlubbers call the crewman a harpooner.

harpoon – a barbed iron spear especially used for hunting whales. Commonly called an iron in the whaling industry.

hatch – an opening in the ship's deck.

hatchway – the vertical space between one hatch and another, for passageway between the decks of a vessel.

heave to – to trim a vessel's sails aback so that it no longer makes headway.

helm – the steering apparatus of a vessel.

hold – the storage area of a vessel.

hull – the main body of the ship.

iron – a whaleman's term for a harpoon.

lance – a spearlike iron pole.

leeward – the side of the ship away from the direction of the wind (opposite of windward).

lifeline – a line stretching the length of a ship to which the crew can hang on when the weather is rough.

loggerhead – a cylindrical piece of wood in the stern around which the whaleline is wound.

luff – to turn a ship close to the wind so that the sails shake and momentum is slowed.

main – the principal, or most important part. In a three-masted vessel, the center mast (mainmast), the center hatch (main hatch), and so on.

marlinspike – a pointed iron tool about 16 inches long, used to separate strands of a rope.

masthead – the top of a mast.

mess – the place where the officers and harponeers take their meals.

mizzen – the third mast, or aftermast, on a three-masted vessel (short for *mizzenmast*).

oilskin – canvas cloth made waterproof by soaking in linseed oil. Sailors wore raincoats and trousers made of oilskin.

old man – the term sailors use when referring to their captain (never in the captain's presence, however!).

pawl – an iron stop used to keep the windlass from turning back.

port – the left side of the vessel while facing forward. Also the designation of one of the watches.

Pull two! – this command tells the two oarsmen whose oars are on the port side to row.

ratlines – the horizontal ropes attached to the shrouds to form a rope ladder (pronounced RAT-lins).

rigging – the lines and ropes of a vessel, used to support the masts and work the yards and sails.

royal – the sail immediately above the topgallant sail.

rudder – a hinged, vertical blade located on a ship's underside at the stern. A ship's course (right, left, or straight) depends on the orientation of the rudder in the water.

scupper – an opening cut in the bulwarks to drain seawater.

scurvy – a disease caused by vitamin-C deficiency, characterized by swollen and bleeding gums.

shipkeeper – one of the people left behind to man the ship while the crew chases whales.

shoal – a sandbar that projects near or above the surface of the water.

shroud – a rope, usually one of a pair, that stretches from the masthead to the sides of the vessel to support the mast.

slop chest – a small store of much-needed goods managed by the captain. Sailors purchased the goods—wool socks, mittens, extra tobacco, boots, etc.—often at inflated prices. The cost was usually deducted from their wages.

sou'wester – a hat made of oilskin, shaped with a broad brim to keep the sailor's face and neck dry while still allowing him to see.

spar – a beam or pole, such as a mast or yard, that supports rigging.

splice the main brace – a slang term meaning "to receive a ration of grog."

starboard – the right side of the vessel when facing forward. Also the designation of one of the watches.

steerage – the living quarters of the shipkeepers and harponeers, usually forward of the officers' quarters.

stem to stern – from front to back.

stern – the back of the ship.

Stern all! – the order to row the whaleboat backward away from danger.

steward – the crewman responsible for the captain's cabin, the officers' quarters, and the serving of the meals.

stove – smashed or crushed, as a boat or ship (past tense of *stave*).

stow – to store.

tack – to change a boat's direction by bringing it head to wind.

tackle – an arrangement of blocks fitted with ropes, used to lift heavy loads.

tiller – a movable bar used to operate the rudder.

topgallant – the sail above the topsail.

topsail – the sail immediately above the lowest sail on a square-rigged vessel.

trypots – enormous iron kettles used for boiling whale blubber.

tryworks – brick structure housing the trypots with water-cooling tanks beneath. Located abaft the forehatch.

tub oarsman – the crewman who sits on the starboard side, fourth from the bow. Oarlock is on the port side. Responsible for wetting the whaleline to prevent it from burning from friction.

tundra – a treeless plain of the Arctic and sub-Arctic regions, with a sublayer of soil that is permanently frozen.

wear ship – to bring a ship around, stern into the wind, until she sails in the opposite direction.

whalecraft – the assorted iron tools used in the whale fishery, such as harpoons, lances, and blubber knives.

whaleline – the rope that leads from the tub to the harpoon, eventually connecting the whale to the whaleboat.

whaler – a whaling ship or bark.

windlass – a horizontal barrel around which a rope or chain is wound. The windlass is turned with a crank and is used in raising heavy loads, such as whale blubber or an anchor.

windward – the direction facing the wind (opposite of leeward).

yard – a horizontal beam attached to a mast to support a sail.

yardarm – the end of a yard.

BIBLIOGRAPHY

ARTICLES:

Kusher, Howard I. "Hellships: Yankee Whaling Along the Coasts of Russian-America, 1835–1852." *New England Quarterly* (March 1972): 81–95.

JOURNALS/LOGS:

Abraham Barker (ship). New Bedford, MA. Sept. 10, 1850–March 14, 1853. Master: Ichabod Norton. Providence, RI: Providence Public Library, Nicholson Whaling Collection.

Abraham Barker (ship). New Bedford, MA. July 21, 1853–April 27, 1857. Master: Abraham Barker, Jr. Providence, RI: Providence Public Library, Nicholson Whaling Collection.

Addison (ship). New Bedford, MA. Nov. 25, 1856–May 27, 1859. Master: Samuel Laurence. Keeper: Ebenezer Nickerson. Providence, RI: Providence Public Library, Nicholson Whaling Collection.

Indian Chief (ship). New London, CT. Jan. 7, 1849–May 8, 1852.

Master: Elisha M. Bailey. Keeper: Elisha M. Bailey. Mystic, CT: Marine Historical Association, Inc.

Peck, Alfred F. July 1856–June 1861. A retrospective journal containing an account of a voyage in an unnamed vessel, probably the bark *Covington* or *Warren* (August 16, 1856–October 1859). Master: Allen M. Newman. Providence, RI: Providence Public Library, Nicholson Whaling Collection.

Smith, N. Byron. *History of a Three Years' Whaling Voyage: Being a true and authentic narrative of the accidents, incidents, and events which happened during a voyage, taken by the author, to the Indian and North Pacific Oceans, in the years 1851, 1852, and 1853.* Kent, OH: Kent State University.

MAPS/ATLASES:

Arctic Environmental Information and Data Center. *Chukchi Sea: Bering Strait—Icy Cape—Physical and Biological Character of Alaskan Coastal Zone and Marine Environment.* Anchorage, AK: University of Alaska, 1975.

United States Geological Survey. *All Topo Maps: Alaska!* Salt Lake City, UT: iGage Mapping Corporation, 2000.

THESES:

Moore, Golda Pauline. "Hawaii During the Whaling Era, 1820–1880." Master's thesis, University of Hawaii, 1934.

VIDEOS:

Hurley, Dr. Frank. *South: Ernest Shackleton and the* Endurance *Expedition.* Harrington Park, NJ: Milestone Film & Video, 1999.

Mystic Seaport Museum. *On Board the* Morgan: *America's Last Wooden Whaler.* Mystic, CT: Mystic Seaport Museum Film-Video Services, 1992.

National Audubon Video. *Whales!* Stamford, CT: Vestron Video, 1989.

National Film Board of Canada. *Champions of the Wild: Polar Bears.* Montreal: National Film Board of Canada, 1998.

New Zealand National Film Unit. *Whales.* New York: Brighton Video, 1988.

WEB SITES:
Chance, Norman A. "Changing Patterns of Subsistence." Adapted from *The Iñupiat and Arctic Alaska.* New York: Harcourt Brace, 1990. *http://arcticcircle.uconn.edu/HistoryCulture/Inupiat/changingecon.html.*

Falconer, William. *William Falconer's Dictionary of the Marine,* 1780 edition. South Seas. *http://www.jcu.edu.au/aff/history/southseas/refs/falc/contents.html* or *http://southseas.nla.gov.au/refs/falc/contents.html.*

Hughes, Charles C. "Eskimo." *http://alaskan.com/docs/eskimo.html.*

International Whaling Commission. *http://www.iwcoffice.org/iwc.htm.*

Lundberg, Murray. "Thar She Blows! Whaling in Alaska and the Yukon." ExploreNorth. *http://www.explorenorth.com/library/yafeatures/bl-whaling.htm.*

New Bedford Whaling Museum. *http://www.whalingmuseum.org.*

U.S. Environmental Protection Agency. "Imprint of the Past: The Ecological History of New Bedford Harbor." *http://www.epa.gov/nbh/html/whaling.html.*

BOOKS:

Albanov, Valerian. *In the Land of White Death: An Epic Story of Survival in the Siberian Arctic.* New York: Random House, 2000.

Alexander, Caroline. *The* Endurance: *Shackleton's Legendary Antarctic Expedition.* New York: Alfred A. Knopf, 1998.

Allen, Everett S. *Children of the Light: The Rise and Fall of New Bedford Whaling and the Death of the Arctic Fleet.* Boston: Little, Brown and Company, 1973.

Ansel, Willits D. *Whaleboat: A Study of Design, Construction, and Use from 1850 to 1970.* Mystic, CT: Mystic Seaport Museum, 1978.

Arctic Institute of North America. *The Alaskan Arctic Coast.* Anchorage, AK: The Arctic Institute of North America, Alaska Office, 1974.

Ashley, Clifford W. *The Yankee Whaler.* 1942. Reprint, New York: Dover, 1991.

Bartlett, Robert A. *The* Karluk's *Last Voyage: An Epic of Death and Survival in the Arctic.* New York: First Cooper Square Press, 2001.

Bockstoce, John R. *Whales, Ice, and Men: The History of Whaling in the Western Arctic.* Seattle: University of Washington Press, 1986.

Bodfish, Waldo, Sr. *Kusiq: An Eskimo Life History from the Arctic Coast of Alaska.* Fairbanks, AK: University of Alaska Press, 1991.

Boeri, David. *People of the Ice Whale: Eskimos, White Men, and the Whale.* New York: Dutton, 1983.

Chance, Norman A. *The Iñupiat and Arctic Alaska: An Ethnography of Development.* Case Studies in Cultural Anthropology, ed. George and Louise Spindler. New York: Holt, Rinehart, and Winston, 1990.

Church, Albert Cook. *Whale Ships and Whaling.* New York: W. W. Norton, 1938.

Cook, John A. *Pursuing the Whale: A Quarter Century of Whaling in the Arctic.* Boston: Houghton Mifflin, 1926.

Damas, David, ed. *Arctic.* Handbook of North American Indians, William C. Sturtevant, gen. ed. Washington, DC: Smithsonian Institution, 1984.

Dana, Richard Henry, Jr. *The Seaman's Friend: A Treatise on Practical Seamanship.* 1879. Reprint, New York: Dover, 1997.

Ellis, Leonard Bolles. *History of New Bedford and Its Vicinity, 1602–1892.* Syracuse, NY: D. Mason and Co., 1892.

Garner, Stanton, ed. *The Captain's Best Mate: The Journal of Mary Chipman Lawrence on the Whaler* Addison, *1856–1860.* Providence, RI: Brown University Press, 1966.

Giddings, James Louis. *Ancient Men of the Arctic.* New York: Alfred A. Knopf, 1967.

Haley, Nelson Cole. *Whale Hunt: The Narrative of a Voyage by Nelson Cole Haley, Harpooner in the Ship* Charles W. Morgan, *1849–1853.* Binghamton, NY: Ives Washburn, 1948.

Hall, Daniel Weston. *Arctic Rovings: The Adventures of a New Bedford Boy on Sea and Land.* Hamden, CT: Linnet Books, 1992.

Harland, John. *Seamanship in the Age of Sail: An Account of the Shiphandling of the Sailing Man-of-War, 1600–1860, Based on Contemporary Sources.* United States Naval Institute, 1984.

Harlow, Frederick Pease. *The Making of a Sailor, or Sea Life Aboard a Yankee Square-Rigger.* 1928. Reprint, New York: Dover, 1988.

Herman, Lewis, and Marguerite Shalett Herman. *American Dialects: A Manual for Actors, Directors, and Writers.* New York: Routledge, 1997.

Hess, Bill. *Gift of the Whale: The Iñupiat Bowhead Hunt, a Sacred Tradition.* Seattle: Sasquatch Books, 1999.

Holmes, Rev. Lewis. *The Arctic Whaleman, or Winter in the Arctic Ocean, being a narrative of the wreck of the whaleship* Citizen, *of New Bedford, together with a brief history of whaling.* Boston: Thayer and Eldridge, 1861.

Howland, Chester S. *Thar She Blows! Thundering Adventures of Whaling and Mutiny.* New York: Wilfred Funk, 1951.

Humble, Richard. *Ships, Sailors, and the Sea.* New York: Franklin Watts, 1991.

Leavitt, John F. *The Charles W. Morgan.* Mystic, CT: Mystic Seaport Museum, 1998.

Lee, Molly, and Gregory A. Reinhardt. *Eskimo Architecture: Dwelling and Structure in the Early Historic Period.* Fairbanks, AK: University of Alaska Press, 2003.

Lever, Darcy. *The Young Sea Officer's Sheet Anchor, or A Key to the Leading of Rigging and to Practical Seamanship.* 1819. Reprint, New York: Dover, 1998.

McCabe, Marsha. *Not Just Anywhere: The Story of WHALE and the Rescue of New Bedford's Waterfront Historic District.* New Bedford, MA: Spinner Publications, 1996.

Melville, Herman. *Moby Dick, or The Whale.* Chicago: Encyclopedia Britannica, 1991.

Mullett, J. C. *A Five Years' Whaling Voyage, 1848–1853.* Fairfield, WA: Ye Galleon Press, 1977.

Munger, James F. *Two Years in the Pacific and Arctic Oceans and China.* 1852. Reprint, Fairfield, WA: Ye Galleon Press, 1987.

Norling, Lisa. *Captain Ahab Had a Wife: New England Women and the Whalefishery, 1720–1870.* Chapel Hill: The University of North Carolina Press, 2000.

Oswalt, Wendell H. *Alaskan Eskimos.* San Francisco: Chandler Publishing Company, 1967.

Parry, Richard. *Trial by Ice: The True Story of Murder and Survival on the 1871* Polaris *Expedition.* New York: Ballantine, 2001.

Pease, Zephaniah W. *Life in New Bedford a Hundred Years Ago.* New Bedford, MA: The Old Dartmouth Historical Society, 1922.

Pease, Z. W., and George A. Hough. *New Bedford, Massachusetts: Its History, Industries, Institutions, and Attractions.* New Bedford, MA: Board of Trade, 1889.

People of the Ice and Snow. The American Indians (series). Alexandria, VA: Time-Life Books, 1999.

Philbrick, Nathaniel. *In the Heart of the Sea: The Tragedy of the Whaleship* Essex. New York: Viking, 2000.

Rennick, Penny, ed. *Iñupiaq and Yupik People of Alaska.* Anchorage, AK: Alaska Geographic Society, 2001.

Ricketson, Daniel. *The History of New Bedford.* New Bedford, MA: 1858.

Robertson, R. B. *Of Whales and Men.* New York: Alfred A. Knopf, 1954.

Shackleton, Ernest. *South: A Memoir of the* Endurance *Voyage.* New York: Carroll and Graf, 1998.

Sherman, Stuart C., et al., eds. *Whaling Logbooks and Journals,*

1613–1927: An Inventory of Manuscript Records in Public Collections. New York and London: Garland Publishing, 1986.

Spears, John R. *The Story of the New England Whalers.* New York: Macmillan, 1922.

Stefansson, Vilhjalmur. *My Life with the Eskimo.* New York: Macmillan, 1951.

Stevens, Rolland Elwell. *Alaska Whales and Whaling.* Anchorage, AK: Alaska Geographic Society, 1978.

Wilbur, C. Keith. *Tall Ships of the World: An Illustrated Encyclopedia.* Chester, CT: The Globe Pequot Press, 1986.

Williams, Harold, ed. *One Whaling Family.* Boston: Houghton Mifflin, 1964.

ACKNOWLEDGMENTS

I would like to extend my sincere thanks and appreciation to the following people: To my fellow writer and fellow Washingtonian Ron Wanttaja for his help with nautical jargon, details, and technicalities; to Michael Dyer, librarian at the Kendall Institute, New Bedford Whaling Museum, for his expert advice on whaling and for his encouragement to "go with it"; and finally to Ann Day at the Tuzzy Consortium Library, Ilisagvik College, in Barrow, Alaska, for providing me with hard-to-find information on pre-contact Inupiat peoples. All opinions expressed in this book are solely mine. If there are any remaining errors, they are my responsibility alone, as to write a story of this nature it often becomes necessary to perform a balancing act between fact and fiction.